for Au
Love your
"Walking Sister

SHORT & HAPPY
(OR NOT)

An International Anthology of Stories

Edited by Richard Bunning and
Dixiane Hallaj

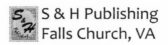 S & H Publishing
Falls Church, VA

Dixiane Hallaj/S & H Publishing, Inc.
211 Park Avenue
Falls Church, VA 22046
www.sandhpublishing.com

Publisher's Note: This is a work of fiction. Names, characters, places, and incidents are a product of the individual author's imagination. Locales and public names are sometimes used for atmospheric purposes. Any resemblance to actual people, living or dead, or to businesses, companies, events, institutions, or locales is completely coincidental.

Book Layout ©2013 BookDesignTemplates.com

Ordering Information:
Quantity sales. Special discounts are available on quantity purchases by corporations, associations, and others. For details, contact the "Special Sales Department" at the address above.

Short & Happy (or Not)/Richard Bunning and Dixiane Hallaj, ed. -- 1st ed.
ISBN 978-1-63320-020-3

SHORT & HAPPY (or Not)
An International Anthology of Stories

Table of Contents

(NOTE: Spelling and punctuation vary by country of origin)

*A short story is a précis: an essential essence,
a sharp quality distilled from quantitative narrative.*

— *Richard Bunning*

SURVIVING A COLD SNAP[1]

Jo Alkemade

Gwyneth ran flat palms along the sides of her face and caught wispy curls between her fingers. She raked her hair behind her ears and leaned forward to glare intently into the depths of the kindling standing near the wood stove. Locals had assured her there was no need to worry about rattlers now, already well into cold season, with snakes deep underground in hibernation. But Gwyneth did not deny her city sensibilities, and the idea of snakes, asleep or awake, appalled her. When she was absolutely positive nothing slithered or crawled down there, she reached into the box.

A dozen or so brittle sticks of kindling left. She might have to go out later, try to get as far as the other side of the hill where the dead juniper bush gave its branches freely. The real worry was the dwindling pile of split logs, and she counted them. Seven. Not enough to last the day. *I guess I'll be breaking legs off chairs next*, she thought doubtfully.

Gwyneth straightened slowly, gently stacking the bones of her back, feeling her age. A good fire would loosen her stiff muscles, and she set about the

---

[1] "Surviving a Cold Snap" was published on Valentine's Day 2014 at http://lesleighkenya.com/surviving-a-cold-snap-by-jo-alkemade/ .

arduous business of building one. Just a few days of relying on its warmth had taught her there was no point in hurrying the process, because that might mean spending a whole morning fussing with a poorly built fire, poking the wood, creating wasteful smoldering without heat. She scraped out last night's ashes, layered grey dry kindling on crumpled newspaper, and leaned flat logs against the sides. She touched a flame to the paper and left the door open, letting air feed the flames, and watched, willing the logs to catch fire.

A slight movement at the edge of her vision caught Gwyneth's eye, and she snapped her head to face it, heart thumping. *Shit*. Was that a mouse disappearing between the floorboards? She thought the pests were nocturnal, but the thick cloud cover had made night and day all but indistinguishable. Gwyneth quickly stuffed another plastic bag into a crack in the floorboards.

She had been cooped up inside this place too long. If it stopped snowing today, maybe she'd finally dig out the old Land Rover, make it to town; buy herself a hot chocolate mocha with extra whip at Starbucks. Talk to one of her distant neighbors, or even a stranger. She dropped her jaw and stretched her lips wide, slowly chanting, *hello, hello, hell-llooo*.

The phone rang, and Gwyneth looked around to see where she'd left it. It glowed on the dining table, too far away to read. Who could possibly be trying to reach her? Only a few loved ones knew she'd fled to this cabin in the boondocks, and she made them swear to leave her alone. It was time to tackle the uncertainties preventing her from getting on with her life. Decide whether her marriage, cooled over the years to corpselike lows, bore the slightest chance of resurrection. The phone stopped ringing.

Gwyneth reheated yesterday's coffee on the stove, and took a cup of it to sit. It smelled charred and she wrinkled her nose in distaste, thinking she might not drink the brew, just let its steam rise to tickle icy cheeks, and warm bluish fingers wrapped around the mug. She looked at the phone and hesitated, wondering whether a voicemail had been left, and whether the message might be important enough to check. Power lines had been down since the storm rolled in three days ago, and now she could not charge the phone. Yesterday a red icon popped up, warning her the battery was running dangerously low.

The wind that creaked and rattled the structure, settled after all this time into a familiar background rumble, suddenly gusted into a huge roar. A thunderous crash shook the cabin, and Gwyneth started, spilling hot coffee over three layers of pants. She did not notice. Freezing air ruffled her hair where wind was finding its way in. Something had broken.

The phone rang. *Not now.*

Gwyneth stood up and cautiously investigated the cabin, searching for the source of the wind. Snowflakes floated lightly in the air, already building a small white pile on the bed covers, and she raised her eyes to see clouds through the holes and cracks of the boarded ceiling.

The corrugated metal roof had torn off.

Her head ducked instinctively at *thump-thump-thump-THUMP*, unmistakable banging, somehow more muted than before. She frowned. *What else is destroyed, if the roof is already gone?* She tried to think, but no explanation came to mind. There was no avoiding it: she must go outside to check the damage. Not that she imagined being able to fix much of anything. She smiled grimly. Another item for the Pro column: *He knows how to wield a hammer.* Followed by one for the Con column: *Never around when I need him.*

She pulled a knit hat low over her ears and forehead, wrapped a second scarf high up to her eyes, added gloves, boots, mammoth polar coat. Gwyneth unlocked the front door – an irrational city habit, this lock, because, honestly, who was going to attack her out here, in this weather? – and pushed hard with both hands. No movement. She put her shoulder to it, leaning with all her weight. The slightest crack appeared between the door and the outside, and a screaming wind forced her back. Just as the door clicked into place, she heard a groan. Or a growl.

Gwyneth questioned the sanity of her ears. She peered through the window and cranked her neck from left to right to see what was happening out there.

On the other side, only the thinnest pane of frosted glass between them, a horrendous brown bear lumbered into view. Gwyneth stuffed both fists to her mouth to stifle a scream so visceral, so

4

undeniable, her lungs almost ripped at the effort. The beast's enormous head swayed and slowly turned, as if it was trying to look her in the eye. It raised one paw, preparing to smash the glass.

The phone rang. Gwyneth sprinted. She tore off her gloves, breath popping out in small jagged bursts. Jabbed a finger at the screen. *Hello!* A burst of static. *Help!* A far-away voice. She couldn't hear. She took a deep breath, forcing herself to focus on the sounds coming from the phone. Battery almost dead. *Help me!* Did she hear her name? *Who is this?*

Another bang shook the house and she turned around. The bear rammed the window again. She froze in horror. The beast raised its paw, ready for the decisive blow. It held up a cell phone. *What?*

Gwyneth ran at the door and slammed it open with the strength of desperation.

Her husband, furred hood gathered tightly around a face swollen and flushed dark with cold, forced chapped lips into a smile. He reached beneath his jacket and pulled out a single rose, crumpled and kinked, stunningly red against the dismal world.

"Happy Valentine's Day," he croaked.

———

After a lifetime of globe-trotting, Jo Alkemade is happily settled in a small town near Santa Fe, New Mexico (USA) with her husband. Jo's novel Belonging in Africa *was published by Lesleigh Ltd. in Kenya. She is currently working on her second novel,* Tires Stuffed with Grass. *Visit* www.facebook.com/Belonging.in.Africa.

DREAM TIME[2]

Lenora Rain-Lee Good

Slowly I turn, step by step and swallow over and over, try to keep the panic that crawls up my throat from becoming reality. I look about me. I no longer know when I am. I no longer know where I am. I no longer know who I am. I look down, and see I stand on sand. Green sand, the color of jade, with the warmth of ice; I look about me again, and see nothing but green sand. My scream becomes the wind as it howls between, over, and around the dunes.

I make it to the bathroom before I lose whatever dinner remained in my stomach. I brush my teeth, wander to the kitchen for a glass of water, and crawl back in bed as Edwin rolls over to embrace me. My scream, loud enough to waken me, did not disturb him at all. I wonder, did I truly scream?

These dreams come more often, and though not on sober reflection in the light of day frightening, at the time of their midnight visits, I am terrified. I don't know of what I am so terrified – I don't remember ever seeing another living soul in any of the dreams, just of my being in strange places, totally out of sync

---

[2] "Dream Time" was originally published in Issue 006 (Sept/Oct 2008), *The Writer's Eye Magazine.* Also appeared in *Dream Time and Other Flights of Fantasy, 2013,* a collection of three short stories by the author.

to all I know. I can tie them to nothing. Not to the news, which I no longer watch; not to foods, which I seldom indulge in; not to alcohol, or books, or visits to the museums. I am a prisoner to my house, afraid to go out, afraid to read, afraid. Period. Afraid of a night phantasm.

Edwin finally senses I am awake and covered in cold sweat. He must love me deeply, as he recognizes the symptom, and pulls me close to infuse his strength and calm into my shaking self. Eventually I open my eyes to the light of day and the sound of the radio.

Dr. Martin tells me I can take control of my dream. That I can face it down, turn to my pursuer and charge at him, or her. Dr. Martin doesn't understand. There is no pursuer. I am alone on an alien world that exists only in my mind. Dr. Martin tells me a lot of psychobabble, none of which is relevant or helpful. He prescribes drugs to help me sleep, but the dreams ignore the drugs and I feel much worse when I eventually waken. I no longer take the drugs. I no longer eat spicy foods or read science fiction or fantasy. I no longer read. I no longer paint. The dreams have turned me into a prisoner.

I determine the next time the dream comes, I will not scream. I will not wake myself, I will see the dream to the end. I swear every night, I will do this. The dream does not come. Perhaps that is the key. Perhaps my mind has no end to the dream and cannot show the picture if there is no end. I begin to breathe normally again. I begin to sleep again. Tomorrow I may pick up a paintbrush, again.

Slowly I turn, step by step and swallow over and over, try to keep the panic that crawls up my throat from becoming reality. I look about me. I no longer know when I am. I no longer know where I am. I no longer know who I am. I look down, and see I stand on sand. Green sand, the color of jade, with the warmth of ice; I look about me again, and see nothing but green sand. I swallow my fear, and decide I am on an adventure. I see nothing alive, so I begin to climb the nearest dune. I quickly learn to climb the dune obliquely, as I seem to slide back two steps for every three I take.

The wind is calm, and the sun is low to the horizon. I have no idea if it rises into day, or sets into night. I reach the top of the dune, and look around. There, away from the sun, is a town. In the low light, the walls of the town appear dark green. A city of sparkling emeralds in this strange light. I see people and animals. I am too far away to see clearly, but feel an urgency to join them.

My need creates anxiety, the fear begins to rise again. I realize the sun sets and I do not want to be on the dune in the dark. I slide down the dune and walk and run as fast as I can to get to the town. It is walled, and as I approach the gate begins to swing shut. I call out and the gate hesitates long enough for me to enter.

I am out of breath. I gulp for air. I taste alien smells. My feet are coated with the green sand.

My breaths are deep, and my heart pounds as I wake. Edwin sleeps beside me, curled on his side, back to me. This time, I do not get out of bed; I do not run to the bathroom. This time, I roll to my back, and stretch, for I have conquered. I do not know if I want to return to sleep, or revel in my newfound bravery and freedom. Sure, now, I am free. I eventually fall back into sleep, and wake with Edwin when the radio turns on.

The village, or town, it may be a city, I had so little time to see, reminds me of some of the photographs of the old desert towns of the Sahara. But the Sahara is a yellow and golden sand, and 'my' desert is jade green. What plants I saw and remember were also different. I can hardly wait to see Dr. Martin and tell him I will no longer need his services.

Dr. Martin and Edwin advise me to continue my visits, though not as often. So now I go once a month, not once a week.

I again paint. My studio fills with paintings of green deserts and blue people wearing bright colored clothes. LeRoi comes, picks out his favorites, and places them in his gallery. Christmas, he tells me, is coming, and people will want something different. He brings me checks and commissions. Never have I been so happy. When Edwin and I go to bed at night, the lovemaking is beautiful, and when I drop off to sleep, I sleep all night.

Slowly I turn, step by step. I am not afraid. Instead of fear, I have a sense of great urgency. I must look and remember. That wall, this shadow, those trees about the well. I must remember the colors, the softness, the harshness. Life flows about me, but no one sees me. Someone touches my shoulder, "Teal? Is it you?" I turn to the voice.

A man, tall, blue skinned, and as handsome as I've ever seen looks into my face. "You've come home! You're back. It is you. Oh, Teal, we've missed you so much." His strong arms fold about me and I am safe. His joy becomes a sun of happiness. But, am I Teal?

"Come, the children wait." We walk through the maze of streets and alleys, to enter a nondescript door. Through the door a courtyard awaits. Fountains spray water, shrubs and trees provide shade and the sand is a playground. Two children, eight and ten, play a form of tag. I watch them, with great maternal pride, as they run and laugh. They see me, stop, then run to me, screaming, "Mommy, Mommy!"

I call them by name, Ceru is the oldest, my daughter. She is beautiful and in a few years will be stunning. Nonday, my son, is the shy one. He waits for his hug, though without patience. He dances from foot to foot in place. I reach out and pull him into my arms.

"Come," my husband says, "dinner waits." We are in the house. It is so familiar and yet so foreign. I must remember. We carry our food to the roof where we eat, enjoy what air chooses to move about us. The talk is family talk, which must be the same wherever there are families. I've never had children, so I don't know. The children are taken down to their rooms and tucked into bed.

Larnay and I return to the roof. "Teal, I don't know if we can bring you again. The planets move and shift in their orbits. The window of opportunity shrinks."

"But, Larnay, I only need to dream and I am here."

"Teal, this is not the dream. You are awake, here. I can prove it." With that, his mouth covers mine. Exactly the

same as Edwin's. And there all comparisons stop. Edwin is gentle and hesitant. Larnay's strength is pure tenderness, his body is mine, and mine is his. There is no hesitancy. His blue skin complements my pink. How could I leave this man, these children? This sex? Satiated, I am on my back, he leans on his elbow and his hand traces patterns on my body. "It will be a boy!"

"What?" I murmur, too happy to care. "Another son. What shall we call him?"

I chuckle and tell him Aday, to go with Nonday. He does not see the humor, and quickly agrees. He reaches over me for a small package I had not seen, opens it, and places a necklace about my throat. "Aday it is. I love you, Teal."

Edwin looks at me with an odd expression. The radio just came on, and he stands at the side of the bed. "Did you dream again?"

"I, I think so. Why?"

"You were restless, and you moaned as if in orgasm."

I blushed. I could feel the color reach my face. "Yes, I think I did dream. These dreams are like an on-going story. They do not pick up each time where the last left off, though there seems to be a sort of continuity. The good thing is I am getting inspiration for painting, and bringing in money. Money for my art. Oh, Edwin, this will be a good Christmas!"

I am out of the shower before I notice the necklace around my neck. It is a talisman of intricately carved Jade suspended on a fine chain of gold. The talisman is to keep the fetus and the mother safe. How do I

11

know this? How do I know Edwin did not place it about my neck as I slept? After all, he did not mention it. I grow very cold, clothes do not warm me, coffee does not warm me.

Dr. Martin tells me I must have purchased it at the little shop in the lobby and forgotten it. He has, he assures me, seen several like it there. I stop at the shop, they have never seen anything like it, but would buy as many as I could get them.

My mornings are horrid. I cannot get out of bed without first eating crackers. Dr. Johns tells me it's normal for morning sickness and should pass in a few weeks. I barely drag myself into the studio. I feel a great urgency to paint. I paint Nonday and Ceru playing in the courtyard. I paint Larnay with them on the roof. I paint the inside of the home, the views and vistas. I paint like a mad woman, and as fast as I paint them, they sell. I paint commissions. People want their children, their faces, in the pictures.

I think Edwin is jealous of my success. He thinks I no longer need him. He says I am too wrapped up in the baby, to the exclusion of him. I try to convince him otherwise. We paint the nursery, it is bright and happy, and Edwin is finally excited, for when the baby comes, we will both need him and all will be right in his universe. I sit in the rocking chair and sing lullabies to Aday; I read him stories. I tell him of his father, Larnay. And wonder how I will explain the blue tint of his skin to yellow skinned Edwin. Then I laugh at how serious I become over a dream, even as a stone of ice forms near my heart. I fear my baby will never sleep in his new crib, that I will never hold him in my arms as I rock in the chair.

My sleep is interrupted only by the need to get up and pee every hour or so. I am grateful I no longer dream. Perhaps Larnay and the children live only on my canvases now, the planets no longer in proper alignment for nocturnal visits. Edwin and our mothers are ecstatic over the nearing birth. I paint feverishly, I know once Aday is born, there will be no time to paint.

All is in readiness for the baby's birth. Aday is due any time now. He has dropped, and I am too miserable to do anything but suffer. I write a letter to Edwin. I tell him how much I love him; how much I appreciate him, and that if anything happens, he is to remarry. That if a choice arises, he must choose baby Aday's life over mine. It is a letter women have written to their husbands, I am sure, for millennia. I hide it under my pillow, so when my fit of melodrama is over, and Aday safe in my arms, I can destroy the letter, and Edwin will be none the wiser.

I turn, step by painful step and swallow over and over. I stumble. I hurt. I am dizzy. Larnay reaches out and catches me. He calls someone, and I am carried to a house and a bed. My face is bathed with cool, wet cloths. My belly flames.

"Her color returns. That is a good sign." I look at my hand — it is blue. I hear voices, but they mean nothing. Larnay holds my hand, gives me his strength. Women try to run him out, but I will not let go. I need his strength, his love. The flame of my belly erupts into a volcano of

13

agony. My screams mingle with those of a baby. Aday is born. I hear congratulations and the word 'healthy' and I sleep.

I wake in my own bed, Larnay holds my hand; Ceru holds Aday, and Nonday looks over her shoulder grinning at his new brother. I know peace and happiness. And the end of those terrible dreams.

———

Lenora lives in the high desert of Washington State where she writes poems, novels, and radio plays. When not writing, she reads, quilts, makes jam, and takes road trips. Her novel, Madame Dorion: Her Journey to the Oregon Country, *is published by S & H Publishing. See* https://www.facebook.com/MadameDorion

THE NIGHT DOCTOR

Ellen Barnes

Wizened and wrinkled, the old woman stood at the bus shelter, like a shriveled brown raisin bent over her walking stick. I edged over on the bench to make room for her. "Is this the G-2 stop?" she rasped.

She was a vision of out of space and time in DuPont Circle's summer heat. The fountain sprinkled crystal drops from the marble Art-Deco pedestal spattering a counterpoint to competing folk guitars and jungle drumming. The year was 1967.

Her voice was faint and scratchy, and I had to strain to hear her words. "Georgetown, y'know," she whispered. "You just missed it. It'll be another half hour," I replied. I edged over even further as she settled into the majority of the bench. I held my breath at the overpowering scent of sweat and cheap perfume. She was dressed in black go-to-church finery and a tatty black sweater, despite the heat. Her stockings were rolled down below her knees and disappeared into sensible shoes, and her blue-gray hair was pulled into a pomaded hot-combed bun. A torn shopping bag rested at her feet. She rummaged through it, retrieving her coin purse. Carefully counting out coins for the bus fare, she began whispering in a sing-song ramble. At first, I wasn't sure whether she was talking to herself or to me, but I listened anyway.

"No child, Georgetown ain't what it used to be. Lawd no! Back when I was a young'un it was surely rundown, wors'n Shaw is now. White folks didn't come near. No suh! Just colored folks. We didn' have no busses then. Uh-uh! Jus' trolley cars an a few mule an' horse carts, you un'erstan'. You think the streets ain't safe today? Huh! They was worse then. You ever hear tell of the Night Doctor? No? Well, when nighttime come, you have to git off the street! Colored folks disappearin'! That's the truth! Right over in Georgetown."

At this point, I interrupted, "What Night Doctor? What are you talking about?" But the woman continued on, ignoring my question.

"Yas, when folks hears that cloppin' of horse hoofs and the cart after dark, they hides! Never seen him m'self, but I heered screams! Why, my aunt knew three folks p'sonnally who done disappeared." She rolled her eyes with remembered fear. "You know, evry'body know, that university on the hill got doctors in trainin'." I made a mental note. That would be Georgetown University, one of our premier medical schools. "An' training doctors need bodies to practice on. Somebody doin' business providin' them. Night Doctor business. Ain't nobody care 'bout some missin' colored folks. Nobody doin' nuthin' to ketch the Night Doctor."

Fascinated, I imagined a sinister figure in black cape and top hat, whip in hand driving his carriage. Horse hooves beating a tattoo on gas-lit, rain soaked cobblestones. Muffled screams…and I shivered.

The G-2 arrived and we both boarded, sitting in separate seats. She sat down filled with proud indignation while I slunk into my seat, shamed with white guilt.

The ride was long and I picked up a discarded *Washington Post* on the seat next to me. My eyes strayed to an article bemoaning the shortage of transplant donors. And I wondered….

———

Ellen Barnes has spent a lifetime stockpiling stories from rich and varied experiences, which now cascade out in writings filled with fact and fiction. She isn't on social media, preferring to be found between the covers of a good book in Round Hill, VA curled up with her cat Claire and a garden full of whimsical wire creatures.

COPROLITH[3]

Ian Lahey

"Dillings!"

Darkness still engulfed the archaeological campsite, vagrant wisps of fog prowled around the tents in the cool night air of the Chilean forest.

"Dillings!!!"

One of the tents shook vigorously and some vaguely human noises could be heard, coming from within. A lantern lit up inside, projecting the silhouette of a startled assistant, dressing hastily.

"Coming, Professor Sukei!" the silhouette shouted back.

Hikari Sukei, Head of Paleontology at Osaka University, had received a generous grant to bring back some specimens for the new museum of natural history, due to open soon, and had taken up the task - Dillings thought - with the single-mindedness of a samurai.

"Dillings, I had that dream again!" the professor said as soon as his assistant arrived, "We are digging in the wrong place!"

"But the mud traps-"

---

[3] An earlier version of "Coprolith" participated in a short story competition on http://www.mywriterscircle.com

"Forget the mud traps! I told you my mother was a psychic, didn't I?"

Dillings sighed. Professor Sukei was an excellent scientist, but had this uncanny and irrational belief in his supernatural sixth sense. "What did you dream of?" the assistant asked.

The professor wet his lips and started describing his dream as if it were a new scientific discovery. Another dinosaur dream. Dillings closed his eyes. Archaeologists often dreamed of visiting their excavation sites in the past, and he himself had more than once dreamed he was a lambeosaurus. Nothing but a dream.

"...fades away." Sukei concluded.

"What?" Dillings asked, feeling guilty for not paying attention.

"I said, dear Dillings, we should get to digging right now, before the memory of my dream fades away."

"Well, worth a try." the assistant sighed, "I'll get the gear."

A few moments later, they left the camp. Sukei in the lead with long, purposeful strides and Dillings, hoisting two backpacks and barely keeping up with him, in a precarious hippity-hop to avoid tripping in the thick underbrush.

"Here! Here is where I saw that pesky scutellosaurus. Did you know their armor looks just like military camouflage?"

"How big was it?" Dillings asked, on these occasions it was always best to humor Professor

19

Sukei.

"Less than four feet, I'd say it was a female."

"Why was it pesky?"

"Well, I tried to touch it and it tried to bite me, a poor excuse for a herbivore I'd say. Luckily I moved my arm just in time, it did snatch my wristwatch though and – Oh! Dillings!!!"

"What?" Dillings crouched in alarm, ready to spring into the Wessmayer Prone maneuver, which is namely to drop at the feet of the aggressor/beast/monster and play dead, hoping the enemy will take more interest in whoever's still standing.

"My wristwatch is missing!" Sukei said, making a show of great surprise and wonder.

"You probably forgot to put it on and left it in your tent." Dillings said, refusing to take the bait. "Isn't the scutellosaurus from Central America?"

"It was, my dear Dillings, until my discovery!" Sukei declared, triumphantly.

"In a dream."

"In, as you said, a dream. But soon to be verified. Come! I remember it ran this way!" The professor bolted through some bushes and Dillings, groaning and loaded with equipment, ambled after him.

He finally caught up with the professor in a small clearing.

"Oh no," Sukei said, "Dillings, this is where I lost it; now I remember."

"I guess he was too fast even for you, Professor." Dillings replied, still wheezing.

"No, I would have caught him, but the T-Rex got to him first!" the professor stared blankly at the empty air.

"What T-Rex?"

"The one that ate my scutellosaurus of course!"

Dillings blinked a few times. "Well, what happened next?"

"I panicked of course, you nincompoop. Have you ever met a T-Rex? There was a large curved rock, hmmm, there! With enough room underneath for me to hide. I curled up and heard the Rex roar, then I woke up with a loud snore. Did you know it sounds like a mix between a foghorn and a fart?"

"Your snoring?"

"No, the roar. Give me the GPS, I need to pinpoint where the rock was."

"Do you want the crew to dig it up?"

"Don't be silly! It would have been dragged away during subsequent glaciations. No, I need to locate this place so we can return tomorrow."

"But your dream finished here didn't it?" Dillings asked.

"Precisely," Sukei replied, "so this is where it'll take up again tonight. I'll see if I can stalk the T-Rex. Let's get back to camp, I want to draw that scutellosaurus."

Hikari Sukei was famous for his accurate illustrations of wildlife and, especially, dinosaurs. Dillings remembered his books from when he was a university student. Half the illustrations bore the mark 'H. Sukei' on them. The professor's rendering of the small armored dinosaur was truly a masterpiece,

Sukei had drawn the beast with such vivid detail Dillings could almost bring himself to believe the professor had actually seen the living, breathing creature.

"That's amazing. The mottled pattern on the dorsal plates looks very natural." Dillings said.

"I'm quite pleased with it," Sukei said, "I bet the Paleontological Society will make a good offer for this one."

"I'm not too sure they'll appreciate the wristwatch hanging from its mouth."

"Well that's what I saw, although I suppose you might have a point. I'll make a watchless version some other time. What's for dinner?"

"Onigiri with tuna."

"Splendid."

Not so splendid, the assistant thought, since Professor's Sukei's entire diet was based on two ingredients: fish and rice. Luckily, Dillings had brought a few jars of his mother's chutney and used it as a dip for the otherwise tasteless rice balls. That night he had the lambeosaurus dream again, this time he was being chased by a T-Rex with Hikari Sukei's face, that kept roaring like a defective fog horn. The beast inhaled once more and opened its maw to utter its predator cry:

"Dillings! I followed the T-Rex!" Sukei's loud voice woke him up. This time the assistant was ready, he had slept with his clothes on and moments later stepped into the professor's tent, both backpacks ready and GPS in his hand.

"Have you seen my watch?" the professor asked. 'Oh, well, it isn't so important. Let's go."

An hour later, they were back in the clearing.

"So this is where my scutellosaurus was eaten, the Rex was on it like a flash. I hid under the rock, as I told you, while it finished its meal. That didn't take long, let me tell you."

"So your new dream really did start off exactly from where it had broken off," Dillings said, somewhat amazed.

"Exactly."

"Wish I could dream serially."

"My mother could do it, too. Anyway, as I was about to say, after the snack the beast went this way. Follow me," Sukei said and almost walked off a cliff. "Woops, the geography has somewhat changed," he said, "it isn't much of a drop, but I guess we'll need ropes anyway."

They lowered the gear first and then climbed down the moss-covered rocks. The professor once more made a big show of concentrating on his dream, reminding Dillings of one of those charlatan fortune tellers he had seen at the town fair back in Leeds, when he was young.

"Now then…. Ummm, yes, the creature went this way, I followed it from a distance, to remain unseen. I think it was suffering from some kind of ailment because as it walked it started making some strange sounds, as if in distress, like this: 'huurrrng, huurrrng'."

"Yes, perhaps it was ill." Dillings said.

"Quite possibly. I'm having trouble because in my dream I followed it around for quite a few hours. Ah! Now I remember! It went towards a rather large bunch of trees in that direction, where that thicket is now." He took off again, without looking behind him. Dillings sighed and shouldered the bags he had just set down, hurrying after the excited professor.

A long trek later, Sukei exclaimed, "Yes! This is the place! The T-Rex finally lay its large bulk here. I saw it roll on its belly a few times, evidently in pain."

"Maybe it had food poisoning. That or it walked itself to death," Dillings said, exausted.

"Interesting theory. Do you suppose our scutellosaurus was poisonous? Frogs in the Amazon rainforest use that sort of defense."

"Killing your enemy only after he's chewed you up is not my best choice of defensive strategy."

"Anyway," the professor concluded, "it was obviously dying. It squatted here and remained still. Then I woke up. Let's get to work, this is the spot."

The assistant produced two telescopic spades. They both began digging. A few hours later it was Dillings who announced he had, in fact, found a specimen.

"What is it? A jaw? A thigh?" Sukei eagerly asked.

"Not exactly," Dillings replied as he held up the large and heavy object which looked like a malformed egg. "I believe this, in paleontology student lingo, is a 'crapstone'."

"Oh, a coprolith," Sukei said, closely examining the fossilized excrement.

"Yup, looks like your T-Rex was dying to take a dump."

"Well," Sukei said, somewhat abashed, "it's still a very good specimen for the museum. Here let me hold – oops!"

The specimen rolled off their hands and fell on the hard ground, where it broke in several pieces. A few small fossilized bone fragments and chewed up armor plates were the discernible remains of the scutellosaurus, but the professor and the assistant's eyes were attracted by something else.

"Well," Dillings said after a long pause, "it took sixty-five million years, but I believe you may have got your wristwatch back."

––––––––

Ian Lahey was born in Milan, Italy, to an American father and an Italian mother. He teaches English Literature and Aviation English in Udine and leads a quiet and ordinary life with his wife, his two children and his invisible cat, Laurelin. To learn more about Ian, visit his FB page: http://www.facebook.com/lovewritingstuff

NOVEMBER

Sherri Fulmer Moorer

It feels like November, Tamara thought as she stared at the darkening sky against the ocean with sad, brown eyes. The wind whipped around the corner of the beach shop more violently than usual, no doubt due to the cold front the garrulous announcers on the radio had been talking about all day. She tightened the rubber band holding her long, brown hair in a ponytail, knowing she had to face that wind if she wanted to find the comfort of home tonight.

Tamara snapped off the radio and pushed a small vacuum cleaner around shelves of sweatshirts and clearance racks of swimsuits and beach towels. *It wasn't like the store really needed cleaning,* she thought as she pushed the buzzing vacuum around listlessly from a sense of dull routine. The summer crowds had left months ago, abandoning the call of the sea for the beckon of the mountains or football stadiums. Their last customers were a young couple three days ago. Newlyweds, they said, looking for lighthouse figurines to decorate their new home with a nautical theme. Tamara sold them the last of the stock at 70% off. *Why not,* she thought. The store would close for the season in two weeks and they wouldn't restock until the grand reopening the week before Easter.

Tamara finished vacuuming and stared out the shop window at the deserted beach. *Did Evan and I look like that couple?* Probably so. The crashing waves reminded her of their time after lifeguard shifts, shop breaks and days off. How many times had they walked that stretch of sand, the sun warming their skin and the salty air blowing through their hair? She lost count as her mind stuck on that last walk on Labor Day. She remembered gazing into his blue eyes in the light of the rising sun, trying to ignore the hum of the car engine in the parking lot behind them. *Going to college isn't the end,* he assured her, *just moving to a new phase of life.* They had something special, or so she thought.

She took her phone out of her pocket and checked it. No calls, no messages.

"It doesn't look like we're going to have any customers today," a voice said. Tamara saw the reflection of Olivia, the store owner, walking out of the storage room and surveying the room with bright green eyes. Her red hair glowed in the reflection on the glass as she picked up a feather duster and swiped it over porcelain figurines of shells and tropical birds, strategically arranged in the front window.

"Doesn't look like it," Tamara agreed, shoving her phone in her pocket.

Olivia frowned. "You haven't heard from him, have you? How long has it been?"

Tamara shrugged as she rolled the vacuum cleaner behind the counter. "Two weeks. Maybe three. He

27

said he was busy with his classes the last time we talked." She stared at the floor and bent to pick up a large, yellow leaf the vacuum cleaner missed. "Maybe he's busy with midterms."

"It's past midterms. Face it Tamara; he's gone."

Tamara returned her gaze to the clouds outside. "I know."

Olivia sighed and tossed the duster behind the counter. "I'm sorry. I shouldn't have said that."

"No, you're right," Tamara said, sniffing. "These things happen. Summer flings, you know. People move on. I should too." She swiped her sweater sleeve across her nose. Her sinuses tingled, perhaps with the start of a cold. "But how? This place dies in the winter."

Olivia nodded. "Be patient. This is a tourist town. Summer always comes and brings plenty of people with it. Who knows? Maybe it will bring something permanent the next time."

"Maybe."

Olivia hit the switch to turn off the "Open" sign. "Closing time, finally. Let's go."

"I don't feel like cooking. Why don't we have supper at the diner?"

Olivia's face pinched. "My husband switched his late day this week. I promised I'd come straight home." She paused and studied Tamara's face. "I'm sorry. I can see you really need the company. Another time perhaps?"

Tamara forced a smile. "Don't worry about it. Maybe we can go next week." She supposed she deserved it. She put Olivia off plenty during the summer to spend time with Evan. "I parked out front, so I'll go out this door. Enjoy your evening."

Olivia switched off the light. "You too. See you in the morning."

Tamara pushed open the door, bracing herself against the wind and drizzle pelting her face. The slap of frigid air sucked the wind out of her, leaving her as grey as the darkening sky. Winter was coming. *Yes,* she thought as she pulled her coat tighter around her, *it feels like November.*

"Excuse me," a voice said behind her. She turned to see a tall man with striking blue eyes and dark hair blowing in the wind. "Can you point me in the direction of Inlet Apartments?" He blushed. "I got lost taking a walk, and you're the only person I've seen since I left the main road."

"That's where I live. Welcome to town, neighbor," she said, holding out her hand. "I'm Tamara."

He took her hand and shook it. "I'm Liam. Nice to meet you." He turned his head up to the sky, where pindrops of rain pelted them. "I guess the storm caught up with me on top of getting lost."

Tamara unlocked her car door. "I can't let a neighbor get caught in this cold rain. Come on, I'll give you a ride." She paused. "Say, have you eaten?"

"No, not yet, and I don't feel like cooking." He paused. "Do you know of any good places?"

"I was going by the Inlet Diner right next to the apartment complex. What say we introduce ourselves over some country cooking?"

"That sounds fabulous," he said, ducking in the passenger side of her car.

She smiled, shutting herself in the driver's seat as the rain picked up. Suddenly, November didn't seem quite so dreary after all.

———

By day, Sherri Fulmer Moorer works in professional licensing; by night she writes from her home in the woods where she lives with her husband, Rick, and her parrots, Zack and Chloe, who find her love of reading and writing stories amusing. You can find Sherri's many novels at: http://www.amazon.com/author/sherrimoorer

OLD BONES[4]

Rob Johnson

YOUR FUTURE LIES IN YOUR HANDS!
Want to know more about yourself?
Want to know what lies ahead?
Then have your palm read by an expert.
Contact MADAM CASSANDRA for a detailed
and confidential reading based on her
twenty years' experience as a professional palmist.
DON'T DELAY. FIND OUT TODAY!
£5 per session.

Ciarán usually ignored the ads altogether, but this one captured his attention as he leafed through the evening paper for the television page. He read it through again and again until his mind raced with visions of the future, with images of a dark gypsy woman, her sequinned headscarf casting a shadow across her forehead as she bent low over a crystal ball. No one believed in all that nonsense, did they? He glanced down at his hands, resting them on his knees and spreading the fingers wide. There were certainly plenty of lines there, criss-crossing his

---

[4] 'Old Bones' appeared in an anthology of short stories for charity called 'Rascals of the Red Barren Bar' in 2010. Published by My Writers Circle and printed by Lulu.com. ISBN 978-1-4467-07838.

palms in an apparently haphazard way, but what did they mean? Did they mean anything at all? More importantly, was it worth five pounds to find out?

Already on the verge of adulthood, the recent dawning of a whole new decade – the 1970s – had only served to intensify Ciarán's increasing preoccupation with thoughts of the future. His past and his present were indelibly stained with the unsettling effects of his Belfast upbringing. The troops on the streets, the slogans on the walls – anti-Catholic, anti-Protestant, anti-RUC, anti-IRA – all were natural features of his youthful landscape, physical manifestations of the unrelenting atmosphere of tension. It was a kind of anti-world, which Ciarán knew to be abnormal but to which he was accustomed. The whole nightmare would have to be resolved sooner or later, but when that would be and what it would mean, no one could be sure. If he could be shown even the merest glimpse of what might lay in store for him, it might help to ease the burden of his deepening apprehension.

By the end of school on the following day, Ciarán had become almost intoxicated with anticipation of a visit to Madame Cassandra. A Pandora's box of possibilities had sprung open inside his head and he had been unable to think of anything else but the instant enlightenment which would soon be his. He hurried off down the street, and all the while he clutched the already battered five pound note in his pocket. The money had been a present for his fourteenth birthday a few days earlier, and he had intended to put it towards a new pair of jeans, but now this shabby piece of paper had taken on a far greater significance. It was about to buy him a vision of his future.

Coming to a halt near the end of a long row of identical red-brick houses, he checked the address on the advert. Surely this was too humble a home for someone called Madam Cassandra. Or perhaps it was a positive sign – a mark in her favour that she was less removed from reality than might be imagined of most mystics.

He knocked and took a step backwards. Now that he was actually on the verge of discovery, a wave of nausea threatened to overwhelm him. Fear of what he might be told about his future mingled with embarrassment that he was putting so much faith in what most people considered little more than a fairground sideshow. He glanced over his shoulder to check that there was nobody about that might recognise him. Half a dozen young boys were kicking a punctured football around, but otherwise the street was deserted.

Stricken with indecision, Ciarán turned back towards the door. With a start, he saw that it was open and a small, white-haired woman was looking blankly into his face.

"Yes?" she said.

He stared into her expressionless grey eyes, partially obscured by the thickness of her spectacle lenses.

"What do you want?" she asked as a frown began to deepen the already heavy lines of her forehead.

He fought for the right words. "Come to see Madam Cassandra," he mumbled.

The woman seemed to relax a little. "That's me sure enough."

"*You're* Madam Cassandra?" As with the house, Ciarán was surprised at the apparent normality of its occupant. There was no brightly coloured headscarf, no large golden earring and no dark gypsy complexion. Madam Cassandra was pale and thin and of the same age and appearance as his own grandmother, and yet there was something about her eyes. At one moment it was as if they barely registered his existence, and at another they appeared to be probing the very depths of his mind. He looked down at the scuffed toes of his shoes. "I've come about the advertisement."

"Ah. So you'd be after a reading, would you?"

The tone in her voice seemed to be mocking him, and Ciarán felt the blood rise in his cheeks.

"Want to know your future, eh? A bit young for that, I'd say. Maybe I should charge you extra."

"Extra?"

"On account you've got more future ahead of you than most who come to see me."

"Five pounds it said in the paper. It's all I've got." As if to prove it, he produced the money from his pocket and held it out in front of her.

"Well, sonny, if five pounds is all you have, then it's five pounds that will have to do." She plucked the note from his fingers and stood back to let him pass.

Ciarán entered the dingy hallway and heard the door close behind him. He followed the woman into the front room where she motioned him towards a small square table beside the window. An overweight ginger cat lay sleeping on one of the two chairs, and she shooed it off. Ciarán sat down and Madam Cassandra perched herself on the edge of the chair opposite him.

"Let's see what we've got then, shall we?" she said with the air of a weary general practitioner about to examine a patient.

She laid her hands on the table and peered into his eyes. He looked away, once more unable to meet her piercing stare, and realised that his palms were damp with sweat. Wiping them on his trousers, he placed them flat on the maroon velvet tablecloth where the underlying threads showed through in several spreading patches. The woman leaned forward and gripped his wrists, gently twisting them so that the backs of his hands were uppermost. She studied them intently for a few moments and then turned them again to inspect the open palms, tilting them this way and that to catch the light.

The silence made him uneasy. He glanced at the old woman's face, the wrinkles of her forehead deeper than before, her unblinking gaze fixed on the hands in front of her. Suddenly, her lips pursed and her eyebrows raised. "Well, you'll surely make old bones and that's a fact. I never seen the like of it. Nowhere near."

"The like of what?"

"Old bones," she said again. "Everything points to it. Clear as day. I'd say you was well on your way to a century. Eighty-five at the very least. – Oh yes, you'll make old bones all right."

Old bones... Old bones... The picture that Ciarán formed – an image of himself, his entire being, finally coming to rest as a dishevelled heap of motley bones – remained obstinately in his head even as he stepped out into the late afternoon sunlight some half an hour later.

In a daze, he made his way homeward, and by the time he reached his own street his irritation was intense. Apart from the woman's prophecy that he would live to a ripe old age, he had heard little else of what she had said. It was as if his mind had come to a grinding halt, unable to travel further than the pile of old bones that had been so abruptly placed in its path.

"Five quid," he kept muttering to himself. "Five quid for *that*." What was the point of knowing he would die an old man if he still had no idea how all those long years would be spent? Perhaps Madam Cassandra had told him that he would marry and have children, that he would be a concert pianist or a doctor or a bricklayer. If she had, then he could not recall it.

"You kept in again?" said his mother as he shut the door behind him.

"What's it to you?"

"Oh that's right. I'm only your mam."

Ciarán started wearily up the stairs.

"And now where you going?"

"To my room."

His mother scowled. "You get more like your dad every day and that's the truth."

"And how would I know?" said Ciarán, and with that he was gone.

He fell backwards onto the bed and stared up at the peeling wallpaper on the ceiling, trying to persuade himself that there must be some value in what he had paid so much to hear. Or maybe he would just have to accept that he had frittered away his entire savings on a whim when he would have been far better off buying a new pair of jeans as he'd originally intended. Not only that, but he had probably committed some sin or other simply by having his palms read in the first place. No doubt there would be a penance to pay on top of the wasted money.

He rolled onto his side and punched the pillow hard. As he did so, he noticed the obligatory print of the Madonna and Child staring down at him from the wall next to his bed. There was something about the Madonna's vacant gaze that reminded him of Madam Cassandra herself. Perhaps that was the answer. Perhaps it was all a matter of believing in what the old woman had told him and having the faith that the true benefit of her words would one day be revealed to him.

And so he began to justify his growing determination to trust in Madam Cassandra's prediction whilst simultaneously making a pact with himself that no one must ever learn his secret. His friends would be merciless in their derision, and worse still, they would also try to undermine his faith – a risk he was not prepared to take.

Although those around him had no clue as to the reason, Ciarán's character visibly changed over the days and weeks that followed. He seemed to have developed a much more carefree attitude to life. He appeared more confident – sometimes to the point of arrogance – but above all, he became increasingly reckless about his physical well-being. It was almost as if he was deliberately putting the old woman's prophecy to the test -- tempting fate, as some might say. Since his visit to Madam Cassandra, he rarely missed an opportunity to demonstrate his bravado, and on the streets of Belfast such opportunities were legion. The British Army was an ever-present and convenient target – a ready-made butt for 'teenage high spirits'. A life-long part of his environment, Ciarán saw the military presence as a matter of fact rather than a political conundrum. All he knew was that the squaddies were fair game. Winding them up was a pastime that came as naturally to him and his friends as kicking a football about in the street.

Armed with his new-found knowledge, Ciarán would always be among the first to arrive on the scene whenever there was trouble. There he would be – right in the front line – hurling bricks and bottles with all his strength and almost taking a delight in challenging the soldiers to respond. On many occasions, they did. Plastic bullets whistled over their heads. Tear-gas canisters exploded in their midst and filled the air with poisonous, choking fumes. The missile throwers needed little further encouragement to scatter. They had achieved their aim, and there was nothing more to be gained by standing their ground. Ciarán, however, was always among the last to flee, still upright amid the chaos, still taunting, still throwing, still yelling. "Soldiers out! Soldiers out! Soldiers out!"

His friends were clearly impressed by his frequent displays of seemingly overwhelming courage, and as his reputation grew, so did his popularity. Ciarán was overjoyed. Never had he expected that the old woman's prophecy would earn him such respect, for he alone was aware of the truth behind his apparent bravery.

***

Madam Cassandra recognised his picture on the front page of the paper immediately. It was almost a year since Ciarán had come to see her, but his youthfulness had made him a rarity in her line of business. She could even remember her emphatic statement that he would live to make old bones.

"We're none of us infallible, to be sure," she said aloud and adjusted the glasses on the bridge of her nose as she held the newspaper up to the light. It was him all right – the features still familiar despite the closed eyes and the stain of blood which spread down the side of his face like an ugly birthmark.

There was a knock at the door. With a sigh, the old woman hauled herself to her feet. "And here's another one with a thirst to know the future," she muttered and slowly made her way into the hallway. As she did so, she clutched at the wall with a dry and withering hand and steadied herself for a moment until the dizziness passed.

"I hear you. I hear you," she called as the knocking came again, and she fumbled for the latch as once more her sight began to fail.

———

Rob Johnson is a Brit living in Greece with his wife Penny, six rescue dogs and three cats. He divides his time between writing and growing olives organically for oil. He is currently working on the sequel to his comedy thriller 'Lifting the Lid'. For more information, please visit Rob's website at http://rob-johnson.org.uk/

FIRST CONTACT

Richard Bunning

The whole of Flight B took off on what would turn out to be a strange day, in the autumn of 1917. Our total complement being six kites including the one I fly. I'm Flying Officer Reg Lyndon, piloting with 2nd Lieutenant Mark Way sitting in as my observer. Our flight of RE8s was equipped for reconnaissance and bombing of artillery installations across the Hindenburg Line.

Everything seemed to be going just top-hole, especially as we were particularly well primed with some ghastly French fizz. The mess hadn't a drop of bitter that week, so we'd made do with liberated liquor. We were in the middle of a right old sing-along when the order to fly was announced. Usual stuff – vital to fly to take advantage of a weather window – an unexpected one, or else I don't think I would have been quite so gassed.

Obviously, Royal Flying Corps pilots never have a tipple before flying. You think so? Whatever, one might officially say that the fumes from the aviation fuel made us appear a little fuddled. Anyway, there is always a shortage of ground crew, so Way, my observer and actually my senior officer, volunteered to swing the prop, and then leap aboard. We had done the same plenty of times before.

Way shouts up to me, "Gas on, switch off, throttle closed."

I shouted, "Check blocks." I'm sure he didn't. Then I went on with the routine, "Fuel on, mixture is rich, magneto off, throttle closed."

Way shouts "First contact" and pulls the prop through, to lubricate the engine.

I reply in standard fashion, "Gas on, contact magneto, half-throttle, ready."

Way bellows out, "Contact" and pulls the prop.

The engine fires, and immediately drags the kite down the lawn. I'm sure I shouted something along the lines of "By Jove, Sir, chocks astray?"

Way makes a desperate run to catch up but never makes it. I'm rolling down the run with other planes behind me, giving me no real choice but to go for it. I curse the bugger for not having secured the kite, but it's too late to worry about that.

Then suddenly, there Way is on a bloody Enfield bike, speeding to catch me up. Smithy, our flight mechanic is driving alongside with Way climbing up to stand behind him.

Next thing I know, Way has jumped aboard.

We are airborne. Way is singing away in my ear, as he sprawls back from his cockpit. I can hear him even above the 4a Engine.

"Oh they say it's a terrible war, oh law,
And there never was a war like this before,
But the worst thing that ever happened in this war

Is Lloyd George's Beer."[5]

I shouted back, "Aye, Way hey up she rises, Sir. You're three sheets to the wind on sacky fizz, remember. We'd better keep to weak government ale in the future."

Two hours later, we are, as usual, blue with cold and only too pleased to be turning the kite back over the lines. We are over our side of the trenches when I suddenly hear Way screaming. I glance around to see him sitting frozen staring off to starboard. The man looks terrified. I look his way only to think my eyes are playing tricks. There's this amazing bank of cloud that looks more like an army of angels than any water vapour.

The next I know I can hear not a sound except that of heavenly trumpets, playing 'Stand Up, Stand Up for Jesus'. The often heard story of the 'Angels of Mons' that many say visited the lines in 1914, comes to mind. Suddenly we are surrounded by what I guess to be similar, if unlikely, apparitions – strange ghostly ships that look to me like devices from a different place in time. Monstrous flying saucers, cigar-shaped airships, and strange flying creatures surround us. Then an instant later, I had over-cooked a turn intended to take us away from these unrecognised formations. The tail flipped out throwing us into a spin. By the time I'd pulled the

---

[5] "Lloyd George's Beer," composed by R.P. Western and Bert Lee in 1915, and sung by Ernie Mayne- 1917.

Harry Tate out and recovered my equilibrium, the skies looked more familiarly empty.

We landed very soon after – or at least we thought so. We were apparently a day to the hour late. What could I report? Everyone knows we had drunk a skinful. My report stands to this day, claiming my official opinion that we were captured in the wires of some great airship, some unidentified flying object of the Bosch. Of course I play up our brave escape supposedly enabled by cutting our kite free with my non-standard issue Elsener 'Victoria' knife. What other cock-and-bull story could we have found to escape being labelled as deserters? Fortunately, the Major, being a thoroughly good chap, preferred to keep our service records in order. He chose to accept our story, burying the details in the fine print of the squadron's records. Was that a first contact with what came to be known as UFOs—a contact we could never officially report?

————

Richard Bunning is a non-fiction being, living in a world of swirling fictions, but his background is mostly harmless, sub-urban and glued in place by conditions which are amongst the best on his planet. See more at http://richardbunningbooksandreviews.weebly.com

I SEE ANGELS

Bobbi Carducci

The first time I pushed through the swinging doors of the Palliative Care unit, I was amazed by the quiet. All the blips and buzzes of a busy hospital were absent. I felt a sense of peace enveloping me; welcoming me. Only then did I understand that my previous assumptions had been wrong. It wasn't a place of death; it was an island of hope and dignity.

Mom was there.

I had come a long way, lugging my suitcase and my fears to sit by her side. I wouldn't leave until she did.

Although it had only been a couple of weeks, it felt as though I'd been there a very long time.

This morning the aroma of fresh coffee lured me to the tiny kitchen across the hall. Grabbing a cream-filled doughnut from the box on the table, I knew right away that Karen was there to see her husband, Bill. Karen always brought us doughnuts. Bill had colon cancer. I hoped to get a chance to talk to her, find out how he was doing before she left again to spend time with their two little girls. She looked up from their glass fronted room and waved to me as I shuffled back to Mom's with my breakfast. It made me self-conscious, and I wondered how much longer I could go before I gave up and washed my frizzy hair in the sink.

Thank God for rubber bands and scarves, I thought. The right scarf and a sassy pair of earrings can go a long way toward extending a wardrobe consisting mainly of jeans, t-shirts and sneakers. I discovered that t-shirts and pajama tops are virtually interchangeable. No one seemed to notice the difference or if they did, well, they were polite enough not to comment.

Mom was finally resting after a twenty-four hour marathon conversation with the universe. Although she rambled incoherently at times, she spoke clearly at others and she took me on an unforgettable adventure, full of a mix of fantasy and poignant memories.

"Wow, look at that!" she said, her eyes wide with wonder.

"I see," I said.

"What is it?"

Uh oh, what do I say next?

"What is it?" she asked again, this time a fearful note in her voice.

"I don't know, what do you think it is?"

"I think it's a bee. I hope it doesn't sting me."

"I won't let it get you. I'll swat it if it comes close again."

"Okay." She sighed, relieved to know that she was no longer in danger.

"Do you have to go on tonight?"

Go on? What was that about?

"I don't think so," I remember telling her. "I'll have to check my schedule."

"I never knew you could sing. When did you learn to sing like that?"

Sing? Me? No way. I laughed to myself. I'm the one they couldn't decide where to place in the second grade choir because my voice is *that* bad. Secretly pleased that she'd given me a talent I always wanted, I wondered if she could also make me a real blonde. Fix it so I no longer have to spend hours at the hairdresser to look more like my beautiful sister.

"Sing to me. Sing me a song so I can rest."

So I sang.

"You are my sunshine, my only sunshine. You make me happy when skies are grey..."

The nurse raised her eyebrows and covered her ears as she went by smiling at the two of us.

I shrugged my shoulders in a "what 're ya gonna do" gesture and continued singing until Mom relaxed in my arms.

"Sleep tight," I whispered, only to see her eyes pop open again.

"Look, look over there," she pointed. "I see angels. Three of them, right over there. They have light all around them, but I don't see any wings."

"Yes I see them," I placated her. "They've come to watch over you as you sleep. Get some rest now, it's okay. You are my sunshine..."

"Oh please," she rolled her eyes. "Stop that racket if you expect me to get any sleep. Who do you think you are, some lounge singer?"

Smiling, I watched as she drifted into sleep, hoping she would truly rest this time, thankful for the gift of song, even if we shared it only for a little while.

We had been up and down all through the long night; I saw her chasing shooting stars, crying over a ruined party dress, livid with rage over some unknown man from her past. I saw the wonder in her eyes as she held her firstborn child. Laughed as she went skinny dipping with my dad in the creek behind their first house. Then for a time she spoke a language no one could pinpoint, growing frustrated with my lack of understanding. Until she looked at me and said, "I love you." I recognize that in any language. Finally, seeing understanding in my eyes, she drifted into a deep peaceful sleep.

As Mom slept, I washed up. After dressing and brushing my teeth, I did my housekeeping. I tossed out the dregs of tea and coffee that had collected in the paper cups left behind by her many visitors. I removed the candy wrappers and fast food cartons brought by her grandchildren. Even in the hospital she couldn't stand to have anyone go away hungry. She loved to watch them eat. I changed the water in the flower vases that lined the windowsill. Everywhere I looked there were cards offering prayers and best wishes for a speedy recovery.

"Your mom is a very lucky woman to have so many people care about her," the nurses told us. "So many of our patients have no one, it's very sad."

They teased us about our big Irish family taking over the place, but I knew they didn't mind.

That morning the man in Room 702 was gone. Just three nights before I'd sat in the lounge watching as his friends went in one by one only to leave quietly trying to hide their tears. Then he was on his way home. A miracle. I wanted one too.

Mr. Wilson next door was dying. His family was with him; his wife sitting quietly holding his hand. I found myself wondering how they met. Did he like to hold her in his arms as they danced the night away? Did they argue a lot? What was their story? The one we all create in the process of living. The nurses drew the curtains. Dimmed the lights and began to whisper as they approached his room.

After a few more hours of sleep Mom woke up. Her mind was clear and she was eagerly awaiting her visitors. My sister was the first to come by, and I left them alone for a while. It was only fair since I got to have Mom all to myself at night.

It was my time to walk in the sun, to breathe in air free of disinfectant. I craved a cigarette. The urge was so strong that if I'd had my purse with me I know I would have gotten a pack, ripped it open and taken a deep satisfying draw only to toss my head back in defiance before I took another and then another. Then I would have coughed and hacked and felt terrible. I was grateful that I'd left my money back in the room. I didn't want to fight that fight again. You'd think that after seven years the urge would be gone. But no, it still hides, stalking me like a cat, waiting to spring out at me when I'm most vulnerable. It didn't get me that day. It was a small victory but one for the win box just the same.

Mom was in her glory holding court when I returned. Her kids, grandkids, some great grandkids all were competing to entertain her. She was opening cards, reading them aloud and laughing.

Her nurse asked to speak with my sister and me. We were the designated spokespersons for the family. The doctors had decided to release her in the morning. Either to a nursing home or to us but there was nothing more they could do for her there. "Home," we told them. She was going home. I'd stay with her and all of us would attend to her needs. We arranged for hospice care to assist us.

We thought we were ready for this but we weren't. My sister and I made the announcement and excused ourselves for the rest of the afternoon. We dusted and vacuumed Mom's house; put clean sheets on the hospital bed now sitting in the den. We ordered flowers to be delivered late the next day. We stocked the refrigerator with all the things she liked and all the supplies we'd need to feed her constant stream of visitors. We went out to lunch.

"Where have you been?" Mom demanded, as I walked into her room. Her visitors were all gone and she was alone in the dim room.

"I went to buy groceries for the house."

"I don't need any damn groceries. And get that tray out of here. The smell is making me sick."

Feeling chastened like the little girl she used to scold, I picked up her tray and carried it out to the kitchen. I called for her nurse and she was given some medicine for the nausea and slipped into sleep once again. I turned down the lights and let her rest. Opening a Power Bar for dinner, I passed the evening chatting with the night nurses.

"Hey, I'm hungry. Where's my breakfast? Are you people trying to starve me or what?"

I couldn't believe it. It was Mr. Wilson. He was wide awake and sitting naked in his bed.

"Get me some pants!" he demanded. "I'm not going to sit here in some stupid gown all day. Where's my food? Bring me some coffee too, with cream not that powdered stuff either."

As the aides scurried to get him clothed again, an order was put in for a breakfast tray. Calls were made, and his family began to arrive.

Mom's skin had a mottled look to it that morning and she was not waking up. Sometime during the night she had slipped into unconsciousness. They had changed places. Mr. Wilson was better. Mom was dying.

I placed a call to my sister. The family gathered once more. The nurses dimmed the lights. They began to whisper as they approached her room.

We could hear the Wilson family laughing, and the flowers being delivered. He was reading his get-well cards. They glanced in as they passed by, indicating sympathy and understanding with a nod before dropping their gaze.

Her chest was barely moving; her expression peaceful. I wouldn't be taking her home after all. Slowly her eyes drifted open, her gaze touching briefly on each of us until finally it came to me.

"I see angels," she whispered. "Three of them, right over there."

"I see them too," I whispered back. "They're surrounded by light and don't have any wings."

Some may doubt what she saw in that moment, but I knew they had come to offer her peace and I had let her go. I searched her face for confirmation.

She nodded and I whispered, "I love you," in a language only we could understand and then she quietly slipped away.

Hours later, tears streaming down my face as I prepared to leave her room for the last time, I felt her presence and a growing sense of peace. I knew that when I went through those doors again, she would be with me always.

As I glanced back through a gap in the now curtained observation window, I was comforted to see three angels — nurses without wings, gathering around her bed.

———

Bobbi Carducci is a multi-published freelance writer. Her stories and her book for young readers have received multiple awards. Her latest book is Confessions of an Imperfect Caregiver *(Open Books Press). To learn more, visit* www.bobbicarducci.com. *Bobbi's blog for caregivers is* http://theimperfectcaregiver.com.

TAKING FLIGHT

Caroline Doherty de Novoa

Why couldn't she be fearless, like the others? But it's not natural to throw yourself backwards into the sea. Water is dangerous, didn't they know?

She was eight when she fell in that river. Slipped on the grass, still glistening from the previous night's rains.

Underneath, everything is a brownish grey. Sounds are unrecognizable. It's when you surface that the panic really sets in. When you hear the water's roar and you know it will devour you again.

CPR, a passing farmer and his Alsatian saved her.

But that river growled through twenty years of dreams.

From the luminous Caribbean water, her husband calls up, "You can do it."

"These fish better be fucking beautiful!" She shrieks before falling.

Hysteria, thrashing around, then calm. Through her mask she can breathe, she can see clearly.

She's floating high above a strange, colourful planet, watching its inhabitants go about their daily business.

Later, back on the boat, she says, "It's like flying, isn't it?"

———

Caroline Doherty de Novoa grew up in the Northern Irish countryside. Over the years, she has called Manchester, Madrid, Oxford and London home. She lives in Bogotá, with her husband Juan. Her novel Dancing with Statues, *is set in Northern Ireland and Colombia. Connect with Caroline at* <u>www.carolinedohertydenovoa.com</u> .

UNHAPPILY EVER AFTER

Ellen Barnes

My name is Cinderella, and I have AIDS."
"No!" Audible gasps could be heard around the circle of the Fairy Tale Princess's Support Group. Cinderella adjusted the tiara nestled in her long, blond tresses. She had never gotten used to wearing it. A tear rolled down her rosy cheek. "Yes, I thought we would live happily ever after. All the sages and magicians foretold it. I'd been losing weight, coughing a lot, night sweats, you know. So I went in for a check-up and the blood test they gave me came back HIV positive. I confronted Prince Charming with the results and he merely shrugged and said I must have cut my foot on the glass slipper and become infected.

The Prince had seemed so distant lately, and then I found him in bed with my wicked step-sister! For all I know, he's been with half the kingdom." Murmurs of sympathy could be heard in the room. "And I don't know what will become of me. If the Prince throws me out, I won't have a place to stay or any health insurance! I have no work experience or credit. I suppose I could go back to being a domestic – that's basically what I was before I married the Prince, but who would hire me under these circumstances?"

"Thank you for sharing, sister Princess." The group leader called for volunteers to share. "Snow White?"

"My name is Snow White, and I am very depressed." Snow White's chin began to tremble and her saucer-blue eyes filled with tears. Someone passed her a box of tissues. "I haven't felt well since I ate that poisoned apple. My Prince is always complaining that I'm no fun anymore. I am expected to sit and look lovely all day long and sing merry little tunes." She shook her glossy black curls. "I don't feel like singing. I feel like crying. And the seven dwarfs are always asking for money. I went to the Royal Physician, who didn't understand at all. He told me how every woman in the kingdom would love to be in my position. He gave me a script for Prozac, but it didn't help. If I'm not feeling suicidal, I'm feeling homicidal." Some group members nodded their heads with understanding.

Another beautiful blond princess spoke up. "My father is a chronic liar, and he told the king I could spin straw into gold. The king locked me up in a room and on three occasions forced me to spin progressively larger amounts of straw into gold or be put to death. I don't even spin flax into linen thread very well and, naturally, I was terrified. But then a horrid little man appeared and spun the straw into gold for me. He was really quite troll-like. I had to keep my mouth shut, of course; my life was at stake. In return for his help, the creature demanded my first-born child. Of course I agreed. What else could I do? Besides, I wasn't even married or contemplating it." She took a deep breath before continuing. "Well, the king was so delighted with his new source of gold he decided to marry me to his son. I don't even think my opinion was asked, but I was profoundly relieved and my life *did* change for the better. I now have an adorable baby girl, but this horrid little man returned and threatened to take her from me unless I could discover his name. It took all of my resources to find out that his name was Rumpelstiltskin, and his fury at my discovery was so great that he stamped his foot and shriveled up into nothing. That was a great relief until I realized that the straw he spun into gold for me was once more straw. The king and the prince are furious. The king is talking about invalidating our marriage. The prince is particularly angry at me for lying, but I was caught in a no-win situation. Now, I'm faced with becoming a single mom and I have no place to go."

The other princesses did not have children, but they clucked their sympathy.

Gerda, of the Snow Queen story, was dressed in white furs and shivering despite the heat. She told through sobs how she thought she must be frigid. Ice. "You don't know how awful it is to be thought of as a cold bitch. I can't seem to melt the heart of Kai, my love. It must be my fault. Everyone thinks fairy tale problems have simple solutions. 'See a sex therapist,' they said. I want to communicate, but it's not working," she wailed.

"I think you princesses have it all wrong," said the Danish princess ballerina as she pirouetted in her pink tulle. "Why, my Steadfast Tin Soldier is the kindest, sweetest, most generous — "

Several voices interrupted, "Well, it's obvious *you've* never been married to a prince!"

"Yeah, and your soldier's handicapped. It's not the same!" cried another.

"Ladies! Princesses! Let's calm down. We're here for mutual support. Everyone here is entitled to her own opinion; and remember, what's said in here stays *in* here!" the group leader raised her voice to be heard.

The door to the meeting room flew open and Mata Hari strode in, gauzy veils streaming behind her, oriental spice fragrance filling the room, clashing with the timid florals of the other princesses. Her smoky black eyes flashed.

"She doesn't belong here!"

"This is a closed meeting!" Shrill princess voices came from every direction.

"Ah, but she does!" replied the group leader. "She was born in a palace in Indonesia, which sort of qualifies her as a princess, and her story is fabled, so hear her out!"

Mata Hari strode into the middle of the group. "You princesses are a miserable bunch of wimps!" she shouted. "What's wrong with you? No prince is going to make it happen for you! You have to be responsible for your own feelings! Look at me! *I'm* my own boss! *I* make my own decisions. Take control!"

Fearful emotions played across some of the faces of the princesses. "But you were jailed and executed as a spy!" cried a princess.

"Right," said Mata Hari. "So I made some bad decisions. But they were *my* decisions and *I* was in control. That's freedom!"

The meeting became chaotic and the group leader called for order and the princesses were gradually drawn into a discussion. At length a committee was duly formed and the first order of business was to conduct a survey of little girls about their aspirations when they grew up. Snow White and Cinderella were assigned to canvass the 25th Street playground. They questioned the little girls playing there. "What would you like to be when you grow up?" The little girls invariably responded, "We want to be fairy tale princesses, just like you, and live happily ever after!"

——

Ellen Barnes has spent a lifetime stockpiling stories from rich and varied experiences, which now cascade out in writings filled with fact and fiction. She isn't on social media, preferring to be found between the covers of a good book in Round Hill, VA curled up with her cat Claire and a garden full of restored whimsical wire creatures.

A FRAGILE WORLD

Tahlia Newland

Crash! Boom!

Thunder shakes the house, vibrates through the old floorboards and widens my eyes. It's right above me. I stare out the window into the suddenly wild night.

Lightning flashes bright against the night and illuminates the grey sheets of rain pouring from the sky – as heavy as if a giant emptied a bucket over the house. It thumps on the tin roof and in the background, the creek roars as the water rises. Merlin, my cat, sits curled up in his basket. He lifts his head and stares through the window. His eyes widen as a flash of light turns the garden silver and another crash of thunder shakes the house. I won't be going shopping tomorrow. The flood-way will be impassable.

The lights go out. Damn. Some tree over the lines no doubt. And my torch is a good stumble away. I move in time with the lightning, thinking how helpful having no curtains is right now. I don't need them up here in the bush. My nearest neighbours are a kilometre away. Curtains would just close me off from the beauty that surrounds my house; only wombats, wallabies and birds are around to look in. The feral goats don't come close enough.

I grab the torch from its re-charge station. There'll be nothing in the wires to re-charge it until the emergency services sort out the tree and the power people fix the lines. I shine it on the floor and find my way into the studio. The floor to ceiling windows reveal the full glory of the storm. Jagged lightning, pounding out a rhythm between flashes, skips over the tree tops and pirouettes off rocks, while rain and wind jerk the strings on puppets of shining leaves. The windows remind me of a series of huge video screens showing a slightly different version of the same event — the power of the natural world. For all that humankind can do, we're still at the mercy of storms and floods, drought and disease, earthquakes and tsunamis.

In the storeroom I find the old kerosene lamp kept for just such times. It's empty. I curse myself for not following my protocol of filling it after each use so it is always ready for emergencies. The kero is in the shed — of course. So it's gumboots and umbrella time. I struggle into the boots, raise the umbrella and tromp into the night, leaving a wide-eyed cat staring through the storeroom window after me. 'You wouldn't like the rain, kitty cat,' I mutter.

The noise in the tin shed is deafening, and the dusty tools and boxes of junk look spooky in the shaft of torchlight, but I find the kerosene bottle easily, and it's half full. I note there's no extra bottle — something to add to the shopping list for when the stream drops enough for me to drive out. I juggle the umbrella and the bottle of fuel in my dance to exit the veranda-less tin shed and shiver when water trickles down my neck. Who choreographed this damn dance? Oh, yeah, that's right; it's improvised, and therefore dangerous because you never know how it will turn out.

The water racing down the stream bed is so loud that rocks and trees are probably rolling down it. I'd like to have a peek, but it's too dangerous. What if my torch dies? I hurry back to the house and splash through water where there shouldn't be any. A blocked drain. Great. They're only ever blocked when you need them!

I drop my umbrella under the car port, open the door and slip the kero onto the storeroom bench. Merlin races through my legs and runs outside. Damn cat. I do not need to be chasing him in this weather. Still, Merlin never goes far. A flash of the torch reveals him sitting and staring at the water rising rapidly onto the concrete. Leave it too long and it will be lapping at the back door. I scoop him up, drop him inside and close the door in his indignant face.

Clearing the drain would be fine if the outside light worked, but with an umbrella in one hand and a torch in the other, it's practically impossible. The torch I need, but the umbrella has alternatives. I either have to don full wet-weather gear, or strip off. It's not cold, so I strip off and dive into the rain stark naked. Cold water pounds on my scalp and shoulders, soaks my hair in an instant and dribbles down my face and over my breasts. I throw up my arms, turn my face to the sky and spin around, giggling like some mad woman. The storm consumes me, and I love the energy of it. But it's not *that* warm, and I don't want to be here long enough to get chilled.

The water is up to my calves already and is too murky for the torch to shine through, so I have to feel around for the drain. My hand scrabbles over rough concrete and a clump of leaves and dirt—that's it. I scoop the debris out with one hand and deposit it on the grass. The water begins to drain. Three scoops later, my fingers feel the grate. I yank it off, clear the muck from just beneath, then whip the grate back on and leap under the car port. Water flowing down a drain is a beautiful sight, especially when it wasn't flowing a moment a go, but I don't stay. I need to get warm.

Back inside, I wrap my dressing gown around me and fill the lamp by the light of the torch.

A short time later, the kerosene lamp sits on the table sending its golden glow into the room. Merlin watches me from his bed.

'What?' I say.

He yawns, stretches his front paws, then settles down for a nap.

I carry the lamp into the bathroom and turn on the shower, grateful that it's gas with a pressure-operated ignition system—no electricity needed—and as I go through the motions of showering, I realise how fragile this modern world is.

Light, heat, transport, food storage, communications, manufacturing; all are reliant on this one thing—electricity is our Achilles heel. It wouldn't take much to bring us down. A huge solar flare would do it, and though rare on that kind of scale, they do happen. It could happen. And it would plummet our world into chaos. Without electricity, everything falls apart.

I hope it doesn't take them too long to get the power back on.

———

Tahlia Newland, author of the multi-award-winning Diamond Peak Series, is also an editor, a reviewer, and a mask-maker. She lives in an Australian rain forest with her husband and a cat. Parts of this story appear in her metaphysical novel, Prunella Smith: Worlds Within Worlds.

I'D RATHER DIE

Dixiane Hallaj

His body lies in an impossible position. Blood seeps into the tiny cracks of the pavement and spreads in an ever-widening pool. Someone in the background screams hysterically. An arm goes around my shoulders. I try to break free.

"It's all right, honey." The voice is low and calm, almost in my ear. What's all right? Nothing's all right. He's broken and no one can fix him.

I feel a blanket wrapped around my shoulders and hands turn me around. I have no breath in my lungs, but at least the screaming has stopped. I am pushed, led, half-carried to a black and white. Why are they taking me to a police car? I haven't done anything wrong. The world slowly comes back into focus. A policewoman lowers me into the seat and stoops to take my hands and talk to me. She asks me the same things over and over. I think I answer the first time, but she doesn't hear me and asks again. She keeps saying "I know this is a difficult time, but..." and asking me questions. I try to answer, I really do, but my answers sound disjointed — even to me.

"Can I read this back to you?" I nod. She begins to read. "You and your fiancé, the uh..." I can almost feel her reluctance to say the words. The deceased.

The victim. The broken object on the street. I nod again. "You and your fiancé," she starts from the beginning, "were walking along the sidewalk talking about wedding plans." She looks up from her notes and waits until I nod. "Then he just jumped out into the street right in the path of the truck."

"Yes," I say. My head is tired of nodding.

"He didn't trip." I almost smile. A person can't make a right turn into the middle of the street by accidentally tripping over a crack in the sidewalk. That's even more preposterous than the truth. "He didn't say *anything*?"

"No. He was beside me one minute, and then he was in front of the truck." I get a mental replay of my glimpse of the driver's face through the windshield. Eyes wide and mouth open, he did what he could to stop. Now that I think about it, I'm sure I can still smell the rubber of his tires over the faint coppery smell of blood.

A large policeman approaches and "my" policewoman draws him away from the car to talk in private. I take the opportunity to look around. The truck driver is being helped into the back of an ambulance. His face is crumpled and covered with tears. His shoulders shake and I hear sobs. Why is he crying? It wasn't his fault.

I whisper to myself, "This is Fred, my fiancé. Have you met my fiancé, Fred?" I'd practiced the words. I'd practiced the casual walk and gestures I used at the annual office party as I moved from group to group showing off my handsome catch. Some of my

SHORT & HAPPY (OR NOT)

co-workers struggled to keep the surprise off their faces. Everyone loved him. Mother loved him. Who wouldn't love a guy who agreed with every word you said? Seriously, every word. It wasn't *such* a bad personality flaw, was it?

Maybe it was too soon to put him on parade. Maybe he wasn't ready. Why couldn't he just send an email and break the engagement? Why did he always have to do things the hard way? And why did he have to do it on this ghastly street, in public? How can I go on, knowing that he'd rather die than marry me? How can I go on, knowing that I'd rather he died than not marry me?

Mother will only remember he loved me.

———

Dixiane Hallaj lives in the small town of Purcellville, Virginia, with her husband of 53 years and their cat named Dog. She has four novels published by S & H Publishing, Inc. More about Dixiane at http://dixianehallaj.com *and* https://www.facebook.com/DixianeHallajAuthorPage

THE VIEW FROM 3½ FEET

Wendy Wong

Ms. Benjefield was a model teacher. In fact, if you looked up the term *Kindergarten Teacher* on Wikipedia, chances were, a photo of Ms. Benjefield would pop up. This being said, Ms. Benjefield had a most unassuming nature and so if you Googled her name, it was unlikely that the search engine would find any mention of her at all.

Nestled in the heart of the city, surrounded by office towers and concrete condo blocks was Ms. Benjefield's domain. The kindergarten class of Woodland Junior Public School was Ms. Benjefield's private enclave where innocence was sheltered and young minds nurtured. The classroom, situated at the very end of the school with its own pint-size bathrooms, dress-up corner and sandbox was removed from the rest of the world. It even boasted its own fenced-in playground to protect Ms. Benjefield's children from the bullies and bigger kids of the upper grades.

On this bright sunny morning, Ms. Benjefield looked down at the children seated before her and smiled that benevolent *teacher smile*, she had mastered so well over the years.

"...And so, Mama Bear, Papa Bear and Baby Bear all gave each other a big bear hug and lived happily ever after," said Ms. Benjefield, as she closed the book.

A dozen little hands sprang up into the air.

"Ms. Benjefield!"

"Ms. Benjefield!"

"Yes, Julia?" she said pointing to the little blond angel in the front row.

"What if there was no Papa Bear – just a Mama Bear and a Mom Bear?"

"I have two Daddies" piped in Christopher.

Ms. Benjefield hesitated for a moment before answering. As she opened her mouth to speak, little Annie answered for her.

"My grandma says it's a sin to have two Daddies or two Mommies, but she's old so my mom says we should just nod politely even when she doesn't make any sense."

The children all nodded wisely in knowing agreement.

Feeling a little in over her head, Ms. Benjefield decided it was time to change the topic.

"Does anyone have anything to share with us for Show and Tell?"

"I do! I do!" Mikey said waving his hand frantically in the air. "I brought some of my Dad's balloons. See? Each one comes in its own little package, but they're not very colorful and they don't blow up very big."

It took a moment to register but when it did, Ms. Benjefield almost swallowed her tongue. "Yes...uh... well...uh Mikey, does your Daddy know you have ah... his...uh...balloons?"

"Nope. I just grabbed them from his night table, but he won't mind. He has lots of them."

"Well, perhaps you should ask before you take things," she admonished gently. "I know. Why don't you leave them with me and I'll send them home to your Mommy and Daddy with a nice little note." Ms. Benjefield scanned the upturned faces. "Does anyone else have something they'd like to share?"

"I have a new dress," volunteered Brigita. "My mom got it at the second hand store – but that's a secret. I'm not allowed to tell anyone about her new Chanel purse either. Mom says it's a knock-out but it looks very real."

"We got a new car," Jason said, "... but the car company took it back because the brakes are sticky. Dad says it doesn't matter because Mom doesn't use the brakes very often anyway."

"I wonder if our new car had sticky brakes and that's why they used a tow truck to take it away," said Jimmy. "My Mom said that if my Dad didn't drink all the time, they wouldn't have had to take the car back. Maybe he spilled something sticky on the brakes."

"I have a new baby sister." Mathew interrupted. "I wanted them to take *her* back, but my Dad says the stork has a *no return* policy. I tried to feed her my broccoli but she wouldn't eat it either." With a big sigh, Mathew shook his head in disgust over his parents' lack of foresight. "If she's just gonna lie there, and she won't even eat my vegetables – why do we need her anyway?"

Ms. Benjefield noticed Sarah sitting quietly at the back of the group. Sarah was a somewhat reclusive child who needed a little prodding every once in a while to get her to participate in the class discussions.

"Sarah is that a new sweater you're wearing? Did someone special make it for you?"

Sarah nodded solemnly "The wicked witch of the east," she answered. "That's what my Dad calls my Grandma because she lives in Scarborough. Daddy goes golfing whenever she comes to visit."

"My Grandma says my Dad is going straight to hell because he hasn't been to confusion in over three years," announced Kimberly. "Confusion is when you sit in that box in the church and tell God and the man everything you did wrong."

"My Daddy doesn't go to confusion either," said B. J. Singh. "He plays golf like Sarah's Dad. Hey! Maybe our Dads can go golfing together sometime."

"Yeah! That'd be cool." Sarah approved.

"My Daddy went to confusion once, but he called it a tax audit."

"What's tax?"

"It's when the sign says your ice-cream cone is a dollar, but the lady at the cash register makes you pay a lot more."

"So then, what's an audit?"

"It's confusion."

"Do you pray when you go to a tax audit?"

"Oh yeah! I know my Daddy did. A lot!"

"Children," Ms. Benjefield spoke up over the growing din. "Remember last week, we talked about bringing stories for our Current Events Corner. Does anyone have a news story that they can share?"

Kamika raised her hand. "We had a man shot dead on our street last night and a bullet came right through the wall by my bed, but I was in the bathroom when it happened so I didn't get to see it."

Ms. Benjefield swallowed an involuntary gasp.

"I bet it was a gang war," said Nathan. "My Dad says we should let 'em all kill each other and good riddance."

"Ms. Benjefield," Laura asked. "If wars are so bad – why do we keep having them?"

"Uh…well…that's…"

"It's because of this guy called Ben Lodden," said Johnny.

"There's a Ben on my soccer team but I don't think it's the same guy. He doesn't fight very much but he did pee his pants once."

The children giggled at poor little Ben's expense.

"I know," Ms. Benjefield said brightly. "Let's sing a song. What shall we sing?"

"The McDonald's song! Ms. Benjefield, can we sing the McDonald's song?"

"Did old Mac Donald have a chick chick here and a moo moo there so he could use them to make McNuggets and burgers? What kind of noise do French fries make, Ms. Benjefield?"

"I like the toothpaste song better," proclaimed Max Jr.

"Can we sing the Tidy Bowl song Ms. Benjefield?"

"My Mom says you can't believe everything you see on television – unless Oprah says it. Mom says Oprah should run the country instead of politicians."

"My Dad says that all politicians are crooks. Is that true Ms. Benjefield? If it's true, why don't they ever go to jail?"

"Yeah! My Dad says they're robbing us blind."

"My Uncle Joe went to jail, but he's not a politician. He's just a car thief."

"Does he know Oprah?"

A migraine was looming. Ms. Benjefield sighed. "I think it's time for our snack."

"Can I have two cookies Ms. Benjefield? I'm kind of hungry 'cause we didn't have much for dinner last night. My Mom went to the food bank but they didn't have very much."

"I had a great dinner last night!" Peter announced proudly. "My Nanny gave me chips for dinner – but I had to promise not to tell mom that her boyfriend came over and that they – "

"Oh dear look at the time!" Ms. Benjefield jumped in. "Time to pack up children. Gather your things and put your coats on. All of your Mommies, Moms, Daddies, Dads, Grandmas and Nannies will be waiting."

"Not mine, Ms. Benjefield. My Mom's at work...but that's okay, I wear this key on a string around my neck. If I lose it, there's another one under the flowerpot by the front door. "

With practiced skill, Ms. Benjefield coaxed and cajoled her children to gather up their belongings and sing their good-bye song. When the last coat was buttoned and the last shoe was tied, Ms. Benjefield gave each little head a pat... and watched the future walk out her door.

———

Wendy Wong worked for seventeen years as a copywriter at one of Canada's largest advertising agencies, then went freelance when her daughters were born. Today she lives in Etobicoke, Ontario and writes children's books. She is currently working on her first novel. You can contact her at: www.wendybooks.ca

WALKING

Jane Buchan

They ask if I'm lonely since he died. Up here, they say, it's easy to get bushed. They worry about bears and bugs big enough to carry a little thing like me right off. Mabel Waterhouse moved to town the week after her husband died, they remind me. But I know that well enough.

I was out walking when the movers hefted Mabel's surround sound speakers and her giant screen into their truck, her oldest unhooking that satellite dish faster than he ever moved to mow her grass. Terrified, says her silly daughter Pauline, scared of the break-ins and the vandalism now that big Ed isn't there to chase them off with his shotgun. Ha! Hell would freeze over before he'd use it on anything bigger than a skunk. Let her go to town, I say. Let her sit in her dusty rose pantsuit with the best of them.

If I died, who'd know, they say. I smile and nod. I get a lot of mileage out of smiling and nodding. What does it matter if I die and no one knows? What's so special about my dying that people have to make some kind of fuss about it, as if I'm the only one dying on Planet Earth? I don't say this to them, but I hope I drop in a place I'll be useful, near the coyote den back in the hills. Or in some field that can use my scrawny ass for something better than embalming.

Old Joe was a corker, they say, and I give them another smile, another nod. If I keep up the clown show, they don't suspect a thing. Behind this idiotic smile, I know what I know and so do they. Joe was a son-of-a-gun. My real mate's always been this land. Joe's passing is cause for celebration, and I'm going to have a humdinger. I'm going to walk from here to . . . well, I haven't decided how far. I'll go on and on until I want my bed and my cobalt blue commode and my chipped Bridal Wreath Limoges teacup. I'll go on and on until I've worked every one of his "You can't walk heres," and "You can't walk theres," out of my system.

Thank goodness, the ghouls are packing up. I can't wait to get out that door and onto a dirt road more enchanting than the yellow brick one in that yarn about the kid from Kansas. They mention the pies in the fridge, the roses on the table. Like I'm the one who's dead and don't know a toad from a toadstool.

Jessie-Lynn is the last to leave, my youngest. I hug her and smile and nod and when she asks for the umpteenth time for me to join her in that miniscule flat in Hardwick. I have to bite my tongue so as not to say that my moving would be for her, to fill up her emptiness, not for me. I don't like living in town. I never have. I'm not moving into some shoebox thirty feet off the ground. If I want to be up in the air, I'll build me a tree house.

I've swept and sang and fed the animals like I'm the queen of all creation and when the cement truck rumbles past I'm out the door as fast as a girl of sixteen chases after the handsome plumber's son. The new owners at Mabel's place are adding an extension and today the weather's good . . . a perfect day for filling sonotubes.

When I get to the site, he's already extended the tube up the hill and is making one hell of a racket with the pumper. When the young driver tells me it's his own rig, I tell him the school kids should be out watching his river of cement flow up hill to those tubes. He says they should be helping with his payments. We both laugh to beat the band.

The miserable little mare neglected by the Firths canters to the fence line for carrots. We're old friends and as I feed her I promise that one day soon I'll be back with tin snips and she and I will canter off into the sunset together. She stares at me with wide, trusting eyes. I guess she knows that now Joe's gone, our departure date is just around the corner. Too many of us are penned up these days, I tell her, and when she nods and smiles just as I did at the funeral supper, I can't help but laugh.

With the sun sliding past the western wood, I walk past Mabel's neighbors to the old Stark place. Some painter's renting but spends more time in Boston than he spends staring at these trees for inspiration. Some people like to say they live in the country, but they haven't got the guts to really do it. They only play at being alone up here. When it comes right down to it, they miss the noisy craziness of all those people jammed into too small a space.

This place knows what it's doing, always has. All the creatures who can't take the space and the silence and the black nights vanish. All that's left are the rooted things, the critters that burrow and feed in secret places until they become the secret places themselves.

A shadow crosses my path. Those long legs and tufted ears tell a story. I've seen a lynx only once in all the years I've lived up here, and that was in the back of Virgil Allen's truck when he drove into town to brag about catching what'd been killing Margie Vanderhaus's sheep. I didn't know myself until I saw the way he'd flung the big cat in the back of his filthy pickup, her long legs draped over Jim Beam bottles, her muzzle pushed up against bear traps. I didn't know until that very day what a hater I could be.

This cat is scrawny but alive enough to turn a square-jawed face in my direction before she disappears. My legs threaten to buckle. I stare into the woods hoping to catch another glimpse, longing like I've longed for nothing else for the big cat to rematerialize. I stand for a minute or an hour, I'm not sure which. And then I'm in the woods, bracken brushing against my shoulders. Nobody hears me coming.

Wild turkeys pecking at the edge of the old Stanley field murmur over dinner until the nearest is hot terror in my mouth. She batters my tongue and gouges my muzzle, but I don't let go. Bones break.

Flesh tears. I haven't eaten in days. She goes down easy, mud and shit and all. Feathers lay in tufts on the bloody ground. Survivors, sisters, cousins, scream their way into the trees. I lick my chops for a second course but they've flown too high. Even if I climb, they'll out wit me now they know I'm here.

A truck's rumble pulls me back into that other body, the one most people around here call Vi. I move to my knees, pretend interest in a ditch full of daisies. "You all right, Miz James? You want a drive home?" Tom Wilbur's boy stares down at me from his new red pickup. Already a prisoner of how things seem, he sees an old woman on her haunches far from home.

"I'm trying not to die of kindness, Billy. You get the picture?" He scratches the stubble on his chin because he's too polite to ask if the sun's got to me. "I'm fine, Son," I tell him, my voice as gentle as his Grandma Pearl's. This is the answer he needs. He can pretend now. He'll say he saw me on one of those excursions I used to make when I was creating show-and-tell library talks for the little ones. Wildflowers and butterfly larvae and birds' nests, my old-lady version of Mother Nature magic.

His truck rumbles to life just as a snarl escapes my lips. I turn away, make sure he can't hear what I've become. I know what's good for me. My knees complain, but hold me up. And then I'm walking again. Walking.

––––––

Jane Buchan, a transplanted Canadian, has lived in Vermont's North East King/Queendom since 2002. She is the author of Under the Moon, *a novel exploring the limiting attitudes to aging. Learn more about Jane on her website* http://www.winterblooms.net .

TRIP UP[6]

John Byk

Johnny Andrealphus rode into Mass City on a bright July day in a white, late model Chevy pickup with a rusted camper top stuffed with clothes, bedding, and fishing gear. Michigan's upper peninsula in the summer is a remote playground for outdoorsmen who regularly pass through its small towns without attracting much attention. So when Johnny stopped for lunch at Grandma Byrd's, the only restaurant in town, nobody gave him a second look except for Maija, the new waitress.

As Johnny entered the empty diner, Maija stood in front of the window, staring up at the ridge of Adventure Mountain. The massive, forested bluff towered over the northern side of town. Deep beneath the outcrop was a long abandoned mine that once provided jobs and prosperity. Towering black storm clouds often rolled across the summit unexpectedly and down into town bringing torrential downpours that quickly saturated the clay-based farms in the community. "Mass City Mud" was what the locals called it and it stuck to everything like

---

[6] "Trip Up" appeared as "Fire and Steel" in *Lumpen Rednecks: Short Stories from Michigan's Upper Peninsula* by Conrad Johnson (a *nom de plume* of John Byk), 2012.

quick drying cement.

Suddenly alerted by the door chime, Maija's first impression was of scruffiness. Johnny looked like he had been camping deep in the woods for some time. His light red beard was coming in thick and he needed a haircut. Taking a stool at the counter, he smiled at Maija with serene blue eyes that seemed to mirror the cloudless sky outside.

"Hi! What can I getcha?" asked Maija. "Do you want to see a menu? Our lunch special today is a chicken wrap."

"Just a coffee," answered Johnny, picking up the daily newspaper that a previous customer had left on the next seat. He turned the pages with thick, ash smudged fingers and combed through the want ads with careful precision without looking up again at Maija who couldn't stand being ignored by men. She was a twenty-five year old, former stripper who always and meticulously attached accessories to herself in order to attract attention. Rainbow colored beads clung to her wrists. Silver crescent earrings hung alongside her face. Her nose and tongue were pierced with glass diamonds and she was never shy about revealing the butterfly tattoo etched onto the small of her back when she had the chance. Johnny's apparent aloofness irritated her so she had to ask him, "Are you vacationing in the UP?"

Johnny looked up from the paper with an automatic uninterested smile. "I'm looking for a place to stay." His eyes glanced at the paper again before he continued. "And I might need a job soon."

"Well, sinners are always welcome in Mass City," she laughed as she tossed back her long, golden hair and then bunched it above her head with hands that had fingernails painted with delicate and intricate designs in hoochie mama fashion. Johnny stared for a moment at her ample breasts, obviously accentuated by a stiff underwire.

"I need a room," he said as he sipped his coffee, "But I don't have much money. I've been sleeping in a tent most of the summer." He looked at her for a reaction. Maija grabbed the coffee pot and refilled his cup with a shaking hand.

"What kinda job you looking for?" she asked, noticing the want ads page in the paper.

"I'm a handyman," he said. "My specialty is fixing broken hearts."

Surprised by his answer, she giggled so much that she managed to hiccup at the same time.

"How do you say your name?" asked Johnny looking with his head tilted slightly to read the nametag pinned above her left shirt pocket.

"It's MY-UH," she answered. "Like the Indian."

Johnny noticed the tiny little scars on the insides of her elbows and when she saw him looking too long at them, she turned away and went into the kitchen. The cook, a tall, bored teenage boy with big hands was fingering his iPod.

"Got an order?" he asked her. She shook her head and went back into the utility room, lit a cigarette and took a deep drag off it and thought for a moment before quickly smashing it out and returning to the counter.

"Why don't you go ask the bartender across the street in the Tiger bar about a place to stay?" she said to Johnny who had his face back in the paper.

Sensing her eager interest he lifted his eyes to really look at her for the first time. "*Why not?*" he thought as he said, "Well, thanks for the tip. How about one back from me? Share a drink? I have a bottle in my truck."

Maija bumped into a stacked row of glasses, knocking one to the floor where it broke into shards.

"Fuck," she said in a low voice under her breath. As she bent down to pick up the broken glass, Johnny couldn't help but notice the smooth white skin above her ass, with its provocative tattoo.

"Are those wings on your back?" Johnny had to ask. Maija stood up and smiled at him, tilting her forehead slightly into his face.

"What kind of bottle do you carry in your truck?"

"Wild Turkey," said Johnny. "What time do you get off? Do you wanna join me for a drink?"

"Why should I?" she replied. Her smile froze, but her hard brown eyes pierced into his.

Johnny looked at her hands that were now shaking so much that she tried to steady them by grabbing onto the edge of the counter. He reached over and placed his hands on hers and said, "Because I know what you need."

He let go of her right hand and reached into his shirt sleeve pocket and pulled out a tiny plastic packet and showed it to her for a second before dropping it back in. Maija's eyelids closed halfway, and she took a deep breath. Johnny smiled deeply enough to show his white teeth.

"Come back in an hour," she told him and then cashed him out. He nodded, walked out, and drove away without looking back.

***

The shadows grow long early in Mass City as the sun drops behind the western edge of Adventure Mountain. Most of the townspeople are farmers and early risers, accustomed to finishing work before the day fades. Except for the few logging trucks that roll through town like thunder, little else happens in the late afternoon until the evening's drinkers start to wander into Tiger's Bar to share stories and advice over countless cold beers and clouds of tobacco smoke.

Maija cleaned her station, cashed out the register, and handed the keys to Honey, the waitress on the night shift.

"Anything happen today?" Honey asked, putting on an apron and pulling her long, blonde hair into a ponytail behind her head. The diner was still empty.

"Nah," answered Maija, anxiously glancing out the window, looking for Johnny to pull into the parking lot again. Honey noticed she was in an exceptional hurry to punch out for the day.

"Got a date, baby?" she joked. Before Maija could answer, Johnny flew in off the highway and coasted to a stop directly in front of the diner door. He lifted his wrist and looked at his watch and then at Maija who came out to meet him.

Maija quickly hopped into the passenger side and shut the door. Johnny stared at her profile a second, and she felt his eyes burning into her so she chuckled nervously. "Let's get this straight. You're gonna hook me up, right?"

Johnny smiled closed lipped again and answered, "Yeah, baby."

Honey ran to the diner window to see who Maija was driving off with, but it was too late. All she saw was the back of Johnny's pickup with a decal of a burning red cross centered in the rear window. The license plate was caked in mud.

Johnny seemed to know where he was going, and Maija liked that immediately about him. He acted just like a backwoods boy—sure of himself without being mouthy. She jabbed into her purse, pulled out a smoke, lit it and turned on the radio, listening to the words of the country music:

And the songbird keeps on singing like it knows the score...

Johnny drove a few miles down the highway and then turned off onto a two track that led deep into the Ottawa National Forest. He didn't slow at all on the bumpy, unpaved road and the truck bounced steadily along as Maija's breasts rose and fell in corresponding cadence to the dips and bumps. Johnny noticed the movement out of the corner of his eye and grinned. Once off the main road and under the canopy of trees that choked off the remaining

86

blue sky, the already dull afternoon morphed into rapidly darkening dusk. A bald eagle broke from its nest at the top of a towering birch tree and swooped down and across the path of the truck. Johnny and Maija watched it disappear and then their eyes briefly met in unspoken acknowledgment of nature's providence — an unexpected intrusion into their private thoughts.

"One thing I can tell you is you got to be free," said Johnny, his eyes back on the road.

"What? What?" asked Maija. "What the hell are you talking about?"

Johnny laughed and pulled out the packet of brown powder from his shirt and tossed it into Maija's lap. She fingered it a little, then opened it slightly with her teeth and moistened her little finger before dipping it into the smack.

"Tastes like good shit," she said.

"The best," he said, "You'll fly away tonight. I guarantee it."

He finally stopped the truck on a railroad trestle over a deep ravine and got out and sat on the hood. The sky was ablaze in sunset colors and Johnny stared up into the wooded hills.

Maija, still in the front seat, yanked out a syringe, spoon, and lighter from her purse and cooked the smack until it became watery enough to suck into the syringe. She pulled the bracelet from her wrist up her forearm and around her bicep and made a fist until a vein rose on the inside of her elbow. Working the needle like a pro, she stuck the cold metal into her body and pushed the dope inside her bloodstream, feeling the hot rush surge through her upper arm, into her chest, and up to her mind. Relaxed, she leaned back with her eyes closed and her mouth parted slightly. She licked her lips with a diamond-studded tongue and moaned.

The woods around her seemed to come alive like a bag of popcorn hot on the campfire. She smelled the fresh pine scent carried on the early evening breeze and heard the distant clacking of a dozen woodpeckers, busily digging into the bark of trees. The thin ribbon of river that ran along the bottom of the ravine echoed in the hollows of her memory and she remembered what happened to her cousin Sandy years ago along the banks of this same creek. They found her body, raped, beaten and stuffed in a barrel, stuck against the side of a beaver dam with gigantic, black crows perched upon it. A chill ran down Maija's body and her toes curled involuntarily. A tight pain gripped the soles of her feet and she tried to let out a small scream but nothing happened. She opened her eyes and saw Johnny in front of the truck, standing at the edge of the trestle, his body forming a "Y" with his hands up flat against the rusted iron of semi-circular arch, one of a series that extended from end to end of the bridge. He looked like a picture in a frame of metal as the sky behind him glowed and smoldered, melting in a sunset of molten colors. His face was dark but she could still see his eyes. She had seen them shine blue in the restaurant, but now they looked metallic black that reflected the magenta colors of the darkening sky. She stumbled out of the truck, taking a few steps toward him as he looked at her, smiling wildly.

"You owe me," said Johnny. "Come here."

Maija felt her knees weaken as she stepped towards him. Then suddenly she felt as though the world was fading from her, shimmering. She found herself stumbling through him as though he had turned to nothing but air. She felt herself tumbling then falling fast, feeling an ice cold pressure of air rise against her face and hair until her arms snapped straight out and lifted her gently into the now blackening sky. She looked down and saw Johnny, a mere shadow now, staring up from beside his truck. She turned her arms, amazed to find herself circling the treetops. An escort of black crows circled with her, dipping into the ravine only to soar high towards the rising moon. She reached an imaginary apex and then gently glided down onto the thick branch of an oak tree on the summit of Adventure Mountain. Her escort settled silently on the branches above her. Maija took a deep breath of forest-saturated air and silently stared at the pinpricks of light in Mass City below her. "This trip ain't so bad," she murmured to herself and then closed her eyes.

***

From behind the window inside Grandma Byrd's, Honey checked the ridge for any signs of approaching weather. The diner was empty but she saw headlights coming fast down the highway and slowing down to turn into the parking lot. The bright white shafts of light momentarily blinded her as the vehicle pulled up to the window. She looked away, but two glowing discs remained suspended before her eyes.

———

John Byk often writes under the name Conrad Johnson. A retired teacher of Modern and Classical Languages, he now spends most of his time in northern Michigan. His live, best-selling author interviews, co-hosted by Marta Merajver from Buenos Aires, Argentina may be heard at http://www.writersalive.com.

CAPTAIN'S BARBEQUE

S. M. Kraftchak

Captains, your qualifications make my decision extremely difficult. Obviously, only one of you can command the Starship Nautilus on this highly sensitive mission," Admiral Zynmar said.

Both candidates for the coveted Captaincy snapped to attention. "Yes, Sir!" the two officers replied in unison, before returning to parade rest, perfectly in sync, to wait for Admiral Zynmar's decision.

"I have made my decision." The Admiral scrutinized the two highly competitive rivals. Carns, a human male, seemed born to impress with his sleek muscular build, dirty blonde hair and silver-blue eyes. His rival Agolon, a prime specimen of a Trilen, stood with his three legs positioned a perfect six inches apart, balancing his four broad shoulders. His long face with its exquisite lime green skin accented by his neatly placed black sensicles curling around the sides was enough to make any egglet swoon. Looks alone would sway enough public opinion to ensure approval of the appointment, whichever candidate he chose, but this mission had special significance. The Admiral's primary concern was the candidate's skill at inter-species diplomacy. His choice would have the sensitive task of commanding the first multi-species crew.

"Captain Agolon, I have chosen you to command the Nautilus."

Agolon snapped to attention, barely hiding a smile. "Thank you, Sir. I will not let you down."

Admiral Zynmar extended a human hand to Captain Agolon who captured the offered hand with all four of his. "See that you don't. Report to Sys Ops for your briefing, immediately. Departure has been moved forward to the day after tomorrow."

Agolon, saluting with one hand to the middle of his green forehead and a second pressed to the middle of his abdomen, turned, grinned at Carns, and slapped him on the shoulder. "Better luck next time, pretty boy," he said and then left.

Carns glared at Agolon's back.

"Captain Carns."

The man snapped to attention and saluted the Admiral.

"I also value your expertise, which is why I want you to lead the final systems check of the Nautilus. Need I tell you how important this mission is to both species? Failure would have a devastating effect on species co-operation along our whole chain of stations."

"I understand, Sir." Carns held his salute to his commander; only his flushed face betrayed any emotion.

"Report immediately to Tech Ops," Zynmar said returning Carns' salute.

"Yes, Sir," Carns said and left. Once the door closed behind him, his fists clenched and his whole body stiffened. "Don't worry, I won't let you down. I'll make sure Agolon is *perfect*. There's nothing more perfect than a barbeque," he whispered as he stalked off.

Carns stood at attention in the line of dignitaries watching the Nautilus push back from space dock as she began her 25th flight. He thought to himself how nice it was to see so many gathered to watch his firework display.

As the officers were dismissed, he smiled and turned away, singing softly under his breath. "It's going to be a hot time, in the old town tonight, fire, fire-"

"Captain Carns!" Zynmar's voice halted him in midstride. "Exactly who I was looking for. Seems you get your chance at the helm of the Nautilus after all. Follow me, transport is waiting. Agolon contracted Marovian Spike and we can't count on him to recover."

Carns turned and stared at Zynmar. "But, Sir-"

"Don't have time for your platitudes or thanks."

"But-" Carns' eyes darted around the empty platform, his breathing suddenly rapid.

Zynmar put both hands on Carns' shoulders and pushed, "Move, man."

Five minutes later, the Admiral stood frowning with his arms folded on his chest as he watched Carns shimmer and disappear. He heard triple footsteps approach and then stop behind him. He spoke over his shoulder without turning. "You corrected the sabotaged fire suppression system?"

"Mostly," Agolon said stepping around to face the Admiral. "Fire will be contained to the Captain's quarters, so his barbeque will be perfect."

———

S. M. Kraftchak spends most of her time with dragons, elves, and aliens, yet still enjoys sunrise on the beach, sunset in the mountains and portraying Elizabeth Tudor. She has three awesome daughters, two dogs, and one cat. Her husband is her best friend, harshest critic and most fervent supporter. Writing is her passion.

AFRICAN HEAVEN[7]

Jo Alkemade

My name is Alibaba," the man said in his lilting speech, placing the accent on the first syllable. *AAAAH-libaba.* He pulled back his lips and lifted the corners in an astonishing smile, revealing a row of sparkling teeth. I wondered briefly whether he'd had orthodontic work done; surely no one was born with such a perfectly spaced set of teeth.

"Madam, you can remember this, no? Alibaba. It is my name."

I pursed my lips and nodded. I knew this tactic of presenting a memorable name so tourists would know who to ask for when they finally decided to commit to a safari, or a mask carved from wood. Probably his real name was Peter. I stared at the man, trying to gauge how much of a sap he thought I was, and to what extent his impressions would influence the price.

From somewhere behind the thatched lean-to, a man wearing neon orange socks in his raggedy sandals jogged toward us, clamping a bench under

[7] "African Heaven" was published under the title "Wide Open African Skies" at http://lesleighkenya.com/wide-open-african-skies/ in April, 2014.

his arm. A few feet of slender board had been nailed to two wider blocks of wood, and it sagged in the middle. It did not look strong or stable enough to support my well-rounded American buttocks.

"Ah," Alibaba cried in almost credible surprise. "Do you see? Here is the bench. We will sit under this papaya tree, in the cool shade, and we will talk. It is the way we conduct business in this country."

The bench was placed carefully in the dappled shade of the one tree that grew out of the dusty earth, and Alibaba sat down happily in the middle, with a white plastic binder on his lap. He shook his dreadlocks over his shoulders. Dreadlocks were clearly all the rage; another way to pander to tourist fantasies, never mind that Jamaica was on the other side of the planet, and the traditional style here was heads shaved hygienically bald. Orange Socks took the place on his left. I hesitated, then lowered myself gingerly onto the remaining space, almost against my better judgment. The bench creaked, but held, though half my right cheek dangled in the air and I found myself in uncomfortable proximity to Alibaba. He smelled vaguely of marijuana.

Now that he had me in his office, he quickly launched phase two of standard operations. A studious expression replaced his smile and Alibaba opened the binder. It was filled with colorful brochures stolen from the nearby grand resorts that cluttered the coastal strip, each sheet of paper stamped prominently with the logo of an international chain. He leafed slowly from one to the next, describing in detail the treasures that waited to be admired in lukewarm ocean waters: wildly colorful fish, flamboyant corals, the delicate local octopus. This was not what I was interested in, but I did not interrupt. I waited for him to feel pressured into revealing his best deals. He glanced at me and continued, trying to elicit a response, and spoke with increasing intensity of hikes to waterfalls, nighttime tours to boozy downtown clubs, safaris to see cape buffalo, kongoni antelope, yellow baboons.

Finally Alibaba closed the binder, careful not to crease his brochures. "Madam. You see? Anything, *a-ny-thing* at all you want, we can provide for you. The exact same safaris as these big hotels, only for a good price, a much better price."

I breathed deeply and considered my words carefully.

"Madam? Which safari do you choose?"

I stood up slowly, rubbing life into my stiff back. The two men sprang up, visibly alarmed that their client was going to depart without buying anything. Alibaba held out his hand to restrain me, then thought better of it and spoke again.

"Your name, what is it? Where are you from? *Sprechen Sie Deutch? Parlez-vous Français?*" His voice dropped. "Maybe you want something different, eh? *Banghi,* weed? Or you like some comfort?"

Comfort? This was new. Apparently the rumors of elderly white ladies traveling to the shores of Africa for sex with virile young tribesmen had been true. Comfort, indeed. And I wasn't that old, either.

"*Sikiliza,*" I said, hoping to impress with one of the few words of Swahili I remembered. "Listen to me. I am not new to this place. I lived here many years as a young girl when my father was manager at one of those big hotels, and I am familiar with the things this land has to offer."

"Ah, you have returned to us. This is wonderful! Now you are a tourist," Alibaba spoke hopefully. Tourists usually overpaid.

"Yes," I admitted. "I am only here for a short visit. But make no mistake, I know what I want, and I will not pay resort prices for it. If you charge me too much, I will simply walk to the place down the road where your colleague Prince Handsome also offers excellent safaris." Same brochures, too.

Alibaba sucked his lips to his teeth loudly in disgust. "Our price is the best, always. This thief Prince Handsome will rob you, believe me. Only tell me what you want."

"I want a leopard. Up close."

If Alibaba's copper skin could have allowed him to blanch, I'm sure he would have turned quite pale. As it was, widened eyes and loss of speech expressed his dismay clearly enough. I sympathized with his dilemma - he wanted to close the deal, but knew what would happen if he failed to deliver on a promise. A bad reputation among tourists would ruin his business.

"Leopards do live up in Shimba Hills Reserve, don't they?" I asked.

"Madam, yes. Leopard, sure, sure."

"Well, then. I want you to take me to see some, and get as close to them as you can."

Alibaba had regained his composure, and took a deep breath. "Leopard live alone in the world. So you cannot see *some*, like a bunch of bananas."

"OK. In that case, one leopard will be fine."

"And then, this is wilderness we are speaking of, you understand? It is not like one of your zoos, where you can just walk to a cage and inside a leopard is living, just waiting for you to see him."

"Point taken."

"In any case, there are only very few of leopard in Shimba Hills. Almost none. And you see how it is hot right now, dry season? Leopard are clever. They hide high in the shade of trees, far inside the jungle; they do not come to look for their water or dinner until it is cool at night," Alibaba smiled triumphantly. "And we may not enter Shimba Hills after dark - it is forbidden. By Kenya law."

I wiped my brow, sweat beginning to trickle its way from my scalp into my eyes.

"Why don't you agree to see elephant? So majestic, astonishing, you will never forget such a sight. Or Pumba! You know Pumba: *Hakuna matata...*" he sang a warbled version of the Disney tune that had become the tourist trade beach anthem.

...Asante sana, squashed banana.

I frowned and tried to weigh the situation. Alibaba's scruples probably had no more substance than his wallet, and truth undoubtedly stretched as far as a handful of dollars would take it. If he felt he had

99

the slightest chance of delivering a leopard, he would already be waving his scrappy contract under my nose. On the other hand, this might only be an extravagant ploy to raise the rates.

I was not ready to give up yet.

"How much?" I said. "What's your best price for a leopard?"

Alibaba's eyes bulged in disbelief and he burst into rapid-fire Swahili. I heard *mzungu, mzungu, mzungu*. White person. Crazy white person, probably.

I felt hope start to fade.

"Why, madam? Why do you want this one impossible thing? Look around you!" He gestured broadly with both arms, opening them like wings. "You are in paradise and yet it is not enough. Do you think you are being reasonable?"

I had come so far, invested every penny I owned, and now stood close enough to see the tips of jungle trees beckoning on the horizon. Somewhere inside that thick green world, a leopard had draped its lanky body around a cool branch high up in the shade, gently snoozing, delighting in slight ripples of breeze ruffling his fur. Could my quest to find him possibly have come to nothing?

I spoke slowly. "A long time ago, my father gave me a toy leopard when I was desperately sick, burning up with malaria. He sat by my bedside and told me stories. About leopards. How they are agile and graceful like dancers, but powerful at the same time, with square jaws overcoming the biggest prey. How they can swim and climb, both. To me, they seemed like the most miraculous of animals." My father's stories about the cat with the spotted fur had taken root in my fevered dreams. I had clamped the stuffed animal close, imagining its strength flow into me. Protecting me.

I was mortified to feel the sudden sting of tears behind my sunglasses, and hung my head in silence. Years later, when I left home, I had not bothered to pack the toy. I was in a blind rush to throw myself into the excitement of grown-up New York City, and desperate to leave the ties of childhood behind.

"Please do not worry," a deep baritone voice spoke. "I will take you."

I looked up in surprise to see Orange Socks hold out his hand for me to shake. "My name is Gabriel," he said. "I am the van driver. If there is one leopard in Shimba Hills to be discovered, I will be the one to find him for you." He spoke slowly, nodding his head to accompany his words. "You may have some special reasons for wanting to encounter this particular animal, of that I cannot speak. And I can provide you with no guaranties. But if leopard is willing to come from his hiding place to meet you, I will make sure you are there."

I did not know how to thank this man who had stepped forward as my unlikely savior. I smiled at him and wiped away my tears.

Now that someone else was willing to take responsibility for the safari, Alibaba perked up visibly and set about negotiating the details of our arrangement in a business-like manner. I grilled him about the reliability of his van. He insisted the vehicle was excellently maintained and had recently been fitted with new quality tires brought all the way from Nairobi. I wanted air-conditioning, but Alibaba said there was no such thing in a safari van. The roof would be popped open so passengers could stand and lean out, enjoying a view far and wide, and the cool breeze that kept people more comfortable than the strongest blast of air-conditioning ever could. We negotiated back and forth about the price until we reached an agreement on even that.

"Tomorrow, 7:30 in the morning, at the pickup place outside the hotel gates," Alibaba concluded.

I had one last item to press home. "We will be two people. We will not be asked to share the van with other guests, OK?"

Alibaba sighed extravagantly, as if my irrational demands had worn him out altogether, but truth be told, he probably didn't have anybody else lined up at such short notice.

"Of course," he said.

***

I started down the thin path alongside the road, feeling light on my feet and energetic despite the blanket of humid midday heat that bore down on me. I heard Alibaba cry that I shouldn't be walking by myself, that he had a taxi for hire at a good price. I turned to face him, and smiled. "See you tomorrow," I called, and waved. Alibaba shrugged and went to sit in the shade of his tree.

I paused for a moment to take a tube of sunscreen from my backpack, my skirt rustling in the tailwind of every car that raced by, enveloping me briefly in a cloud of black exhaust. I rubbed cream thickly onto my bare arms and face, and took special care with the tops of my feet and toes. I adjusted my wide-brimmed hat so neither the back of my neck nor the tip of my nose stuck out in the sun, and put my oversized movie star sunglasses back on. The water in my plastic bottle had warmed unpleasantly, but I took a few sips anyway. When I felt prepared to endure the walk without roasting to a frazzle, I continued slowly on my way. It wasn't far to the tiny cottage where my father had been living for the past twenty years.

On the day of his retirement, he had been told to vacate the apartment on hotel premises that had been our home for too many years to count; he knew he could never again live away from the ocean, and rented the best place his meager savings would allow. It wasn't much, and on seeing it, my mother announced she had put up with more than enough years of mosquitoes, power outages, sweating heat, and a long list of other discomforts. She left him. I, in my first year of college at the time, never found a reason to visit. Until now.

I climbed the few rickety steps to the narrow ve-randa that encircled the cottage and pulled open the bug screen, propping it behind my hip as I reached for the door knob. I brushed my hand briefly across the hard flakes of sky blue paint on the front door, and watched them rain to the floor. The door jammed slightly, warped by humid sea air, and I pushed with force until it groaned and let me in.

I removed my sunglasses and waited for my eyes to adjust to the dimness of the room. The shutters were wide open and the long eaves of the thatched roof kept hot sunlight out. A ceiling fan churned lazy movement into the air. I took off my hat and the slight breeze cooled the sweat on my scalp.

My father sat in his wheelchair in front of the window, looking out at the world he was no longer a part of. His nurse left the room discreetly.

"Daddy," I said.

He turned slowly to face me, his eyes sparkling in recognition. I crouched by his side and covered his dry, gnarled hand with my own.

"It is all arranged, Daddy."

My father smiled, but did not give a sign that he understood.

"Do you remember saying there was just one last thing you wished to do?" I asked.

His head, heavy with age, bobbed weakly on the thin neck.

"Remember? It is time. Tomorrow we will go into the jungle to see the leopard. And I will stay by your side. I promise."

My father's toothless mouth opened in a big, delighted smile. He did not stop kneading the threadbare stuffed animal that rested on his lap.

———

After a lifetime of globe-trotting, Jo Alkemade is happily settled in a small town near Santa Fe, New Mexico (USA) with her husband. Jo's novel Belonging in Africa *was published by Lesleigh Ltd. in Kenya. She is currently working on her second novel,* Tires Stuffed with Grass. *Visit* www.facebook.com/Belonging.in.Africa.

TO LOVE AGAIN

Maryann Miller

Gloria hurried into the Starbucks and saw her friend already seated with a latte. She waved, then headed to the bar for coffee. Or maybe she should have tea. Something soothing. Her nerves had been all a jangle ever since the visit from Frederick the evening before. She couldn't wait to tell her friend why he had come.

She ordered a chamomile tea, and when it was ready, took the cup and joined Felicia. Early this morning, Gloria had called and asked Felicia to meet her at the coffee shop, tantalizing her by saying she had the most amazing news to share. Felicia had pleaded for Gloria to tell her straight away, but Gloria put her off, telling her it had to be said face to face.

Now her friend looked over at her, excitement flashing in her eyes. "Okay, now are you going to tell me?"

"This man I know from Sunday school came to visit me last evening."

"Okay."

"Frederick. His name is Frederick."

"Okay." The look on Felicia's face clearly indicated she found nothing so amazing about this. "So what did this Frederick have to say?"

"'I've come to *court* you, Gloria.'"

Felicia stifled a laugh. "Really? That's what he said? Nobody talks like that nowadays."

"That's what I told him."

"What? Your response was to correct him?"

Gloria sighed. "I didn't correct him. I merely pointed out that people don't court these days. According to my grandson people hook up."

"I've heard that, too. Not exactly sure I know what that means."

"Me either. But maybe we're better off not knowing."

Felicia took a sip of her coffee, then asked. "So what did you tell him?"

"I told him I didn't know. I'd have to think about it."

"Well, don't think too long. We're not teenagers anymore."

Gloria stirred more sugar into her tea. "What would you do?"

"Don't put it off on me." Felicia laughed. "This is a decision you have to make."

When Gloria didn't respond, Felicia got up to buy a couple of blueberry scones. She brought them back and slid one over to her friend. "So tell me. How do you feel about this man wanting to *court* you?"

"I'm not sure." Gloria broke open the scone and buttered one half. "I like him. He and his late wife were good friends, so I know what kind of a man he is. He was so good to her when she was sick."

"He sounds like a terrific guy."

"Yes. He is. But we're old. Well past the stage of falling in love."

"Gloria Keith, I can't believe you said that. You who always lives life to the fullest."

"This is different."

Gloria averted her eyes, making a big production out of buttering the second half of her pastry, and Felicia said, "You're scared, aren't you."

"Wouldn't you be? Ray was the only man I've ever loved. The only one I have ever been with. You know, hooked up. What if Frederick wants to... you know."

Felicia laughed. "It's only an evening out. And if he was so formal as to say he wants to court you, I doubt he'll ask you to go to bed on the first date."

"Don't be crass."

Sometimes Felicia could be a little rough around the edges, but that had always further endeared her to Gloria. She'd been taught that ladies don't say bad words or talk about what went on between a man and a woman, and Felicia's openness was sometimes like a breath of fresh air. Despite their differences, they had developed a bond deep enough that allowed Felica to be crass and Gloria to be prim without diminishing the friendship.

"I've got an idea," Gloria said, wiping bits of butter off her fingers with a napkin. "Why don't you and Dave join us for a dinner? I could cook and invite

Frederick over and that way it wouldn't be like a real date."

"But what if he wants a real date?" Felicia grinned. "What if he wants to kiss you good night at the end of the evening?"

Gloria's neck grew warm at the thought. And much to her chagrin, so did another part of her anatomy. "You're being crass again."

"No I'm not. Just think about it for a minute. It's clear he has some expectations. You just have to decide if you have any."

Gloria folded her napkin into smaller and smaller squares. "I just thought that part of life was over. After Ray... you know. I'm almost 70 for Pete's sake."

"Does that mean you just sit in your rocking chair on the back porch and let the rest of your life just blow on by?"

Gloria tried to find an answer, but words failed her.

"That's not the Gloria I know," Felicia said. "My friend Gloria has never been afraid to jump into a new adventure."

All the way home, Gloria thought about what Felicia had said. Was it true? *Am I just too scared to entertain the idea of a new adventure?*

She pulled her little Honda into the detached garage, then walked to her back door. Instead of passing the rocking chair on the rear porch, she paused, thinking she might sit down for a moment. But then again, maybe not. She ran her hand along the back, giving it a gentle push. As the chair slowly rocked back and forth, Gloria wiped her sweating palms on her slacks and walked into the house.

If she didn't call Frederick right now, she might never do it.

———

Maryann Miller, author, screenwriter, editor, part-time farmer, and theatre director at the Winnsboro Center for the Arts, lives in the Piney Woods of East Texas. She has a virtual home at <u>www.maryannwrites.com</u> *and blogs at* <u>http://its-not-all-gravy.blogspot.com/</u> *and is on Facebook and Twitter as @maryannwrites.*

FINAL GIFTS

Jane Roop

The truth about Uncle Bot's whereabouts was unknown to everyone except the twins, Buster and Emma. They stood in the circle with the family around the grave in the McThigh-Wooten cemetery, sad but relieved their mother, Rose, was at last safely in the ground between their dad and Uncle Cotton.

"Too bad we couldn't find Bot," Aunt Jean said. She was a solid, barrel-bellied woman with grey braids layered over her head like a tiara.

Aunt Jean and Uncle Beans, the oldest surviving members and themselves second cousins of the tattered and poor Oklahoma side of the McThigh clan, wiped their rheumy eyes with holey bits of a handkerchief from Uncle Beans' hip pocket.

"It'd be safe for him now Rose's proper gone," Uncle Beans said.

She had been gone in mind ever since her first husband fell off a haystack and broke his neck leaving her with the then seven-year-old twins, a milk cow, a few chickens and a farm to manage. A decade later, her madness blossomed from forgetfulness into nuttiness. She fell from the roof trying to axe aliens coming in through the chimney, broke her neck, and died.

Even Aunt Jean, Rose's sister, had more than once told Bot he'd better move out, come to live at the lake. There was a cot in the living room and a pot of beans on the stove every day, enough for anybody. After all, he was family more than just once over, being not only Bot, their brother-in-law, but Jean and Rose's uncle which made Emma and Buster, Bot's grand-niece and grand-nephew and also his step-children. Bot was a bachelor when Rose was widowed. According to the faithful in the community, it was Bot's biblical duty to marry her having no wife or children of his own.

Aunt Jean tried to get the twins to leave too after Bot went missing, fearing her sister would wake up suddenly one day and not recognize her own children, but Buster and Emma stayed put, bringing in the eggs, milking Sadie, walking the mile down the rutted lane each school day to catch the bus.

"Rose was a good'un with an axe." Uncle Beans said by way of his contribution to the remembrances of Rose. He had a sweet, simple mind. Even the copperheads that slid through the jumble of weeds around his place and curled up in the sun on the front porch were free of harassment, their only intimidation coming from Uncle Beans' scolding voice and stomping feet, "Git along now, you lazy critters, git along."

Emma and Buster agreed with Uncle Beans and Aunt Jean about most things, except the thing about them moving to the lake. Not only were there copperheads, there were water moccasin. Rose, their

112

skinny mother with lighting flashes of madness in her deep-water blue eyes, was less a threat than all those snakes.

With Beans' axe compliment, the twins agreed. Exactly what Buster had said just a few months after they planted Uncle Cotton, Rose's older brother.

"Mother is good with an axe," Buster had said standing in the doorway to Bot's bedroom.

Yes, Emma thought, but the axe buried in Bot's face probably couldn't be counted as good. What were they to do with the bloody, faceless man ? They couldn't call Sheriff Logan. First thing that would happen Mother would be taken away and then they'd be shipped off to live with Jean and Beans, they being the only family close by after Uncle Cotton's passing.

"I guess we could bury him before Mother gets up," Emma said.

"It'd be easy, he's such a little bit. Nobody would know," Buster finished Emma's thought which often happened between them.

Both sets of blue eyes, as blue as their mother's, a trait of the McThigh clan, had been at ease with the practicality of such a solution. Uncle Bot's social security check could still go into the bank. Small as it was, it made life on the farm easier and his money had been part of the deal.

"We did take care of him regular like since Mother couldn't," Emma said.

"It was a right fair contract," Buster tilted his head, the way their collie used to when they spoke to him.

"Bot took care of us and we took care of him. Breakfast every morning." He nodded. "We was good to him. We'll say he left. In a couple of months, we'll be old enough to move into town and get a job."

"Who'd take care of Mother if we leave?" Emma asked not expecting a real solution.

"It'd be time the state take care of her like they did old man Cummings," Buster said.

"Ok," Emma shoved both hands in the pockets of her faded overalls.

"Better than snakes." Buster said.

The family cemetery was a quarter of a mile from the house, mostly uphill.

"Won't be so much digging if we put him on top of Uncle Cotton," Emma said. They looked at the newly turned dirt and the cluster of faded plastic flowers where the family had gathered to bury jaundiced Uncle Cotton, and his over-ginned liver.

"They always liked each other," Buster said.

Even when people didn't like Cotton they didn't say much out of respect for him being a paratrooper during the war and doing stuff nobody wanted to talk about, especially him.

"We got to say a few words," Emma said as she tossed a last shovel of dirt back into the grave.

"He wasn't a bad man," Buster said, "but I got mighty tired of fixing him two eggs sunny side up every morning."

"He was a messy eater, poking the toast in the yoke and dripping it all over himself," Emma added.

"He never..," Buster started.

SHORT & HAPPY (OR NOT)

"hit us," Emma finished.

They stood a few more moments then started with "Our Father".

At the AMEN, Emma said, "At least he got his wish..."

"He died in his sleep," Buster said.

———

Jane Roop is a retired securities broker living in Kennewick, Washington, at the confluence of the Columbia, Snake and Yakima rivers.

O'BUDLIN MATRICENTRICITY

Richard Bunning

Elizabeth (1926-1952), Brenda (1952), Sunshine (1969), Marsha (1984), Rebecca (2002), Elizabeth (2026)

That no-good man of yours isn't going to turn up, is he?"

"Probably not Mum, that's why you're here, remember? And you promised not to go on about Bem."

"Well, yes but, it really isn't good enough. He was happy to get you pregnant."

"Stop this. It was my decision to have a child, not his. You managed fine on your own and I'll be just the same. You're right. **He** really isn't good enough. Anyway, when have fathers ever been more than passing visitors in our family? Even your Grandmother, Brenda, was single with child and in those days bringing up a kid alone really would've been difficult. Ha! For all we know we go back generations as abandoned women. Well, it's possible, your Grandmother never even knew her mum, Betty, did she? You've told me loads of times how Betty died bringing Brenda into the world. Betty wasn't married was she? A housekeeper to the local Catholic priest, nod nod, father Father, wasn't she Mum? Except that the church covered that all up. And your granny, Brenda looked after by the Sisters of Mercy.

Being brought up Catholic in an orphanage did her a fat lot of good, seeing as how she ended up pregnant with Nanna Sunshine at sweet sixteen."

"Yes, you're right Rebecca. That seems to be the way in our family, my mother, born at the end of a rock festival on the Isle of Wight. I know she has a lot of theories about who her father was, or should we say fantasies, but Sunny hasn't a single real fact. And Gran isn't going to ever own up now. Anyway, I bet she doesn't know. The mystery is just a way of hiding her embarrassment. After running away from the Sisters I think my Gran, Brenda, was just surprised and pleased to find a way of getting a warm bed at night. When she climbed over the orphanage wall she was only thirteen or fourteen. I can assure you that Dublin in '66 was no place for an innocent girl to be homeless. You should talk to her sometime about it all. But if you want the truth don't intimate that I put you up to it, understand! She expects her little 'secrets' to remain just that. She had quite an adventure surviving on her own, eventually arriving off the Dublin to Holyhead ferry with Nanna already growing inside her. As for you darling, at least I know who you father is. He really cared for you Rebecca, though he was never going to break up his marriage for us. At least Chris had the decency to help out financially."

"It hasn't been easy for any of you, but you've managed, and you are the best Mum in the world. Well, at least you are when you're not nagging."

"Jesus wept! Five generations, another just arriving and not a father worthy of the name! Especially, noting that holy bastard that was almost certainly my great grandmother's father. He has got to be the worst of men, that wicked priest 'preying' on rather than praying for his congregation. What is it about we O'Budlins? Even our name seems to be an invention; well I've never met any other O'Budlin's did you? What is more, never has a maiden name stuck so long. Or are you going to break with that tradition?"

"No Ma, I'm certainly not; I'm proud to be an O'Budlin, even if it is a name invented for the paperwork of a convent. Anyway, even in 2026 it is better for a child to have her mother's name than that of a never-was father. Chins wag and make life difficult enough as it is, without being labelled by carrying a different surname to one's own mum . . . Agh, huff, huff . . . We know one thing for sure, without doing any tests, don't we Mum. We know this restless lump will be a girl. You could think it was witchcraft, one girl to each generation and always out of wedlock. Nothing changes. I want to call her Betty, after my great great granny. She will be a proud O'Budlin as well. Anyway, Betty Marsha Uzochukwu sounds a bit weird to me. Betty Marsha O'Budlin is much better. Our corny anagram of Dublin is a great big part of whom we are."

"That's lovely dear, Betty after our Coven's oldest known member! Um … very thoughtful, but doesn't Betty sound a bit old fashioned nowadays? Name her straight Elizabeth, after all that was how your great great grandmother was christened. That way she can shorten her name in lots of acceptable ways. Anyway, we're not all girls. Don't forget my brother, your Uncle Robert."

"Well, he's as close to being female as a man can be, isn't he? Anyway, back to what I should call my daughter, avoiding an over-popular name is good, I think. But I get what you're saying and I never knew that Betty was christened Elizabeth. Daft aren't I, not to work that out? Anyway, you can bet that whichever derivative we use, soon as it becomes set there will be an obnoxious drag-queen, or a killer, or some other ghastly character, using the name. Naming kids is such a lottery. I bet Brenda was a common enough name when Gran was born, especially in an orphanage in Galway. But I think it sounds more old-fashioned than Elizabeth or Betty now."

"You're quite right love. As you say, it is often possible to guess the age of people from their names."

"Well, certainly Nanna. Fancy anyone being called Sunshine. I never let on at school that my Nan was a sixties hippy. Have you noticed that nearly every old picture we have of Nan as a child, she has flowers in her hair. Half the men had hair nearly as long and all."

"Yeah, my Mum is an original free spirit, born to the sounds of what we now call Classical Rock and probably the smell of marijuana. She first poked her head out on the 31st August 1969 in the back of a VW

Camper Van, still on the way to hospital. I don't know if it was the Moody Blues or the Who that got her revved up to pop out."

"I've heard of both those ancient bands. That's a clever pun, Mum."

"I know that! Um, what is?"

"Pop music, pop out the baby! . . . I've always wondered, but never had the cheek to ask Gran what a girl brought up by Nuns was doing going to a rock festival nine months pregnant."

"I think that the question has already answered itself. Anyway, as I said earlier, she grew-up very young."

"Ah! Well yes, I see what you mean. I think I would have run away as well if I had been brave enough. We're all a bit the rebel in our time, isn't that right Mum? A right little rapper weren't you! I've seen the video evidence, remember! But hardly as 'right -on' as Sunny! I think I'd have gone a bit off the rails if I had been brought up like Nanna.

"So are you sure about naming her after me? I mean, who's called Marsha? In fact, I was named after Marsha Hunt, who played at that very festival. Nanna wanted me to grow up with that sort of spirit, that sort of drive. Hunt grew up strong in a family of strong black women in a colour divided America."

"I never knew that, Mum, that's really wild. She's black, brilliant? That seals it for me, especially given Bem being the Dad. It's amazing that you ended up so boring then in'it Marshy Babe. Ha, ha."

"Cheeky beggar, but yes, I see what you're saying. You're right, Marsha would be cool. I bet both Gran and Nanna will approve whatever names you choose. You could give her names after all of us. Haha, that'll give her style. Elizabeth Brenda Sunshine Marsha Rebecca O'Budlin. What do think about that?"

"Yeah well, that way none of my illustrious family gets left out. Well, except Uncle Robert."

"Well, I'm surprised at you. Couldn't you add a Roberta? Haha."

"Okay!"

"Noooow, I didn't mean it."

"Ayaa, ah, ah ah, Hold my hand Mother. Bloody Bem, you think that with neither England nor Nigeria still in the World Cup, he might've found time to come. Even if just to pop in to check I was okay. I mean, he only bloody works here, well you know, a mile away of corridors, in A & E."

"Don't fret, you have me. Do you want me to call the midwife?"

"No, not yet! Just pass that bloody gas."

"Jesus girl, you near crushed my fingers."

"Well, hold my hand proper next time."

"Did I ever tell you, your father isn't really British as such?"

"No Ma, not more than a hundred times and him being called Christiano Baros, I'd never have guessed. Talk about a crappy attempt at distraction."

"Okay, that *is* foreign, but lots of folks that are English have foreign names. Though he lived here since he was a baby he was actually born in Athens."

"It's funny how you think I don't remember all you have told me about my real father, Mum. I'm twenty-three, not the scatterbrain child that seemed to be only interested in ponies."

"You'll always be my baby, dear, I can't help the lectures. I bet every mother is the same. He was the boy-next-door, a friend through childhood. I don't know how he seduced me."

"Come off it Mother. You were hardly the innocent young thing. You knew full well he was already engaged, right? I bet you half ripped the pants off him."

"Well, yes. It would be wrong of me to pretend I was unaware of what I was doing. Though, I was childish and extremely stupid to think that he would abandon Trudy for me. He was always decent, and insisted on helping me support you even when we moved in with Tom. Very few never involved fathers would do that. I bet he'd love to see the baby, when you get a chance. I also know that Trudy is totally accepting of you. I don't know that I'd be if our roles were reversed."

"Yes, I'll make a point of seeing them. ... Mum, have you ever thought about the fact your great granny was protestant. I mean, we know that from the Births and Deaths register. But there she was, a protestant in Galway, housekeeper to a Catholic priest. Ow! It's coming on again. Aggh, huuu, huuuu, huuuu .... Pass me that water."

"Breathe darling, big breaths .... That's it .... Yes I have though lots about who exactly Betty was. We don't know for a fact, but I think it's more than likely that her parentage was never known. There always were protestants in Galway, and so I'm sure her story was hardly unique. She was a foundling; according to records, though someone knew something of her background. After all, it was known that she was a protestant child with a name. Perhaps the baby was discovered with a written note in her 'crib' .... It was before her time, but when I did some research on the internet and that, there was a protestant orphanage burnt down in Galway in 1922. So you know; some other arrangements must have been made for the abandoned for a while after at least."

"That's fascinating Mum. I didn't know you'd done research like that."

"Well, there you go, your old Mum isn't a total ignoramus. Can I help you up the bed a bit, you don't look very comfortable?"

"Well, that's a typical Mum understatement. I don't look bleeding comfortable, blimey."

"Lean forward a little so that I can heave up the pillow."

"Arrh! Thanks. Why didn't you ever have more kids Mum? I mean, you were steady with Tom for years. As virtual stepfathers go I could have had far worse. He loved you Mum. I bet he still does."

"Actually you very nearly did have a brother, but I never let on to you at the time. I carried Luke in me for four months. You were fourteen, a difficult age to be faced with a baby sibling."

"Oh Ma! How come you never told me? And, I was so beastly to you at that age. No, you were right. I would've made sure I didn't understand, wouldn't I? You even named him. Luke, that's lovely. That shows how much you wanted him. I'm so sorry Mum. . . .Actually, I'm also a bit angry you never let on. I mean I understand, but it's still like you didn't trust me and that hurts."

"I've always felt close to you. I should've trusted you to get over whatever it is that makes teenagers obnoxious, trusted you to accept facts. But at the time it just didn't seem right to pressure you with it. Then as the years passed I never did feel the time was right to bring the subject up. I guessed you would be angry that I had held it from you."

"You must have been so upset, especially as I was almost out of control then. Just when you needed me as a friend, I was high all the time and even nicking money off you. I don't know what I'd do if you weren't here for me now. Sorry, you've made me cry."

"And now you me! Don't be upset sweetheart. Everything happens for a reason."

Balls shit! But ... but I understand, especially now that I have carried a child. Anyhow, we are almost like sisters now, what with you being only eighteen when I came along. Brenda, will be lucky – two mums, Nanna, and Great Granny to keep an eye. Even Gran's only in her sixties."

"Yes, that's right. She was born in the year that the Queen became our monarch, 1952. What's more, Betty was born the same year Elizabeth Windsor was, 1926. So if she'd lived through delivery she might well still be with us as well. I've just realised, she would be a hundred."

"Hu huhuhuhuhuhuuuuh."

"I really think we should ring the nurse."

"No, no. I'm okay. Huuuh. It's passing. Fucking hell, why do we do this?"

"It's all worth it, you'll see. And hard work though a baby is, they're wonderful years. Well, at least they are looking back, ha, ha. I wouldn't have missed them for the world."

"HaHaHaa. Aggh, don't make me laugh. Talking about looking back, I miss Tom, you know. He really was a good dad to me, despite all the horrible things I said when he left."

"Yes, he was a good unofficial stepfather. He was just a weak man, flattered by any female that showed the least bit of interest in him."

"But none were ever half as pretty as you, Mum."

"Well thanks Dear, though hardly true. Anyway, let my misfortunes be a lesson. Just you remember that the male brain is in the testicles."

"Couldn't you have forgiven him?"

"Yes, and yes I did, a time or two, but he will never change. You know what I think? I think that fathers should be forced to be present when their kids are born. That way surely any but the most selfish would buy into the family thing, would make some sort of connection with their child."

"Or be scared off sex for life. Mind, I'm not sure anything would put Bem off. And shit, I miss him. I don't care how many generations the women in our family have coped alone, I really don't think I can for long."

"I'm sure things will come right, dear. You just wait, you're so beautiful and intelligent."

"I think that's actually some of the problem Mum, men are not psychologically geared to the likelihood of playing second fiddle in the career game. Young ones are scared flaccid by any half competent female, especially ones likely to get on at work. I'm twenty-four but with a good degree and already in middle management. As for that solid ceiling of male bosses that are senior to nearly all women despite years and years of supposed equality; they just want their egos flattered with a quick conquest or two, secure in the belief that their wives will never find out and that women are too stupid to know when they're being exploited."

"Haha Rebecca, scared flaccid. See what I mean. You're such a bright spark with words. But I disagree with my clever daughter. We don't help ourselves in the workplace, thinking merit without push will get us promoted. We women are just as much part of the problem in the marriage game as well. It is just as much the way we are, you know, looking for a superman all the time, when what few top-catches there are to go around are usually only capable of loving themselves. Like handsome dickheads. What's a polite word?"

"Narcissists."

"No, I was right, dickheads!"

"Hahaha, you're right Mum. Arrrgh, huhuhuhuaaarr. Dickheads. Aaaaagh. Now look what you've done. It really hurts Mum. I don't think I can do this."

"You'll be fine, but I'm going to call the nurse."

"Huhuhu. Yes. Call. Hand me that bloody mask."

"Okay, so give me the button, or you press it dear."

"*And stop calling me dear!* Bloody hell, that fucking Bem, doing this to me."

"Now breathe deeply. Relax between contractions."

"You bloody relax ... *Oh Christ! – Bem!* What are you doing here, you bastard? Come here. Give me a hand I can really squeeze."

"I love you too, Reb. Sorry I took so long. I was borrowing the 'suitable car' of Tom. I met him in the pub. He offered it a while back, and anyway I thought it only fair to let him use my vintage Spyder in exchange, and well, I wanted to make sure he could handle it."

"Nice to see you Bem. I think I'll leave you two to it and go and get myself a nice cup of tea. I'll give the midwives a shout as I pass."

"Oh, Mum, I love you so."

"I know dear, and I am so happy to see that it isn't just the O'Budlin coven that loves you."

———

Richard Bunning ascribes to the view that artists don't have to suffer to be creative, but definitely do need to be very nosey about the sufferance of others. Richard's writing and views on others can be found at: http://richardbunningbooksandreviews.weebly.com

ONE SHOT TO BE BORN

S. M. Kraftchak

I will be born five years from now, if I don't miss. The damn temporal guardians refused to tell me why it was so important that I do this myself, other than they had run all the scenarios. Me rescuing my parents had the fewest time echoes and was critical since I had an important part in the future. I almost laughed aloud. That's what they told all of us Time Drifters. They gave me a choice, of course, if you can call it that, but then who else but me could make the shot?

As I winked in on the pier and got my bearings, my mouth dropped open and my bag slipped from my fingers, thudding on the smooth stainless steel. Season's Folly, in this time, wasn't the same ship I knew from the future. My dream of traveling on a posh star-liner burst when I realized my life depended on the antiquated ship in front of me.

"How the hell do they expect me to make it to the other side of the galaxy in this antiquated piece of —?"

"She's a real beau'y, hain't she?" a male voice whispered at my shoulder.

I buried my nose in my sleeve to hide from the overwhelming stench of rotten fish and rancid seaweed. Cautiously I turned to see a man who looked like he'd stepped off an imagination deck where one of those ancient pirate interactive ocean adventures had been playing. My face must have given me away.

"Awe, she hain't that bad. Season's Folly will get you where you're agoin' in style."

"If I wanted a retro glamour-style cruise, I'd have booked an SST not a —"

"Classic SSS? Solar Sailin' Starships offer memorable passage, Lass. You've no idea what you're missin'."

I looked around the empty star-port, chosen for its remoteness. "I think I'm about to find out."

"'ear now, let me get your bag. I've put 'er to ship shape just for you and wiff you bein' the only passenger, we can set sail anytime you wanna."

Only my will to live, or more accurately – be born, and my refusal to breathe even half a lung of the man's odiferous body odor kept me from saying, "How about never?"

***

After 120 hours on board, most of which I had pleaded illness and kept to myself, I'd gotten used to the strange rise and fall motion of the ship. The Captain assured me it was identical to planet-side water sailing ships and in fact, Season's Folly was an exact replica, as near as possible, of the ancient water ship Mandalay. Her sleek white hull was crowned by three masts of stacked white solar sails, rising high above a tinted force dome arching from gunwale to gunwale. As we pulled into port, people on shore pointed at the ship, as we eased into the crowded docks. The temporal guardians had chosen well; the second best place to be unobtrusive was a crowd, even if we splashed into the middle of it.

I knew a back way to the Purple Iguana. Positioning myself in the tournament would be easy. I just had to make the shot. If I made it, the prize would assure *I* would disappear from the ill fated cruise, if not, *my parents* would and I'd just wink out of existence.

"Jumpin' jellyfish, Lass, I almost didna' make you."

"Thanks, that's the point," I said and hitched at the wide strap that held a long black slender case slung onto my shoulder.

***

The Purple Iguana was better than most Fozzbool halls and smelled like an extra coat of paint had been slapped onto its walls to make it ready for the big tournament. I avoided as many people as possible, Drifter policy, by keeping my own company in a small corner booth. In the early half of the tournament, taking advantage of the overconfident Fozzbool sharks hardly seemed fair, but I eased my conscience by making it look hard. As I moved up the brackets, I might have sweated one or two shots, but smiled as the final bracket on the standings board lit up- just me and him. There'd be no cockiness in this game – my life depended on it.

As I grabbed my cue and turned, I met the eyes I knew so well. I tipped my head and spilled my straight bright auburn hair across half my freckled face to avoid recognition, although I don't know why since there was no way he could recognize me (since I technically hadn't been born yet), and clasped his offered hand. It was warm and engulfed my hand just like when I was a little girl.

"Andromeda Fatz. Sorry I can't take you with me on the cruise. It'll be my Honeymoon with that cute red-head over there."

I glanced at my future mother, who could have been my sister, and shook my future father's hand. "Gemini Gin. Sorry you'll have to settle for Blarney Beach for your Honeymoon," I said knowing full well that's where they had gone.

"Huh, ha, ha!" Father's hand landed with a smack across my shoulders. "We'll see about that," he said and led me to the glowing Fozzbool display in the center of the hall. "Ladies first."

The room quieted as we circled the 3D-holo-Fozzbool, assessing the game. Best of three limited our exhibitionism to bouncing off the pulsing force field pegs and a number of less than spectacular shots, as far as I was concerned, even though we each shared the crowd's favor equally. I played it safe by using just the edges of the simulated gravity wells and took the first game; he took the second with a risky shot and we were deep into the final winner-take-all game. My parents' lives, not to mention my own, depended on my next shot. As I walked around the display contemplating the position of my last holo-ball, I click my cue on Mother's wedding band that I'd worn since she died when I was ten. I almost giggled at how much fun it would be if I winked out in front of everyone when I missed. I shook my head. No fun there, I wouldn't be here to see it. Whispers from the crowd brought my mind back to the game as I climbed three steps to get to the top of the glowing blue display. I decided I'd shoot down across the center gravity well, a truly spectacular shot.

Whispers turned to murmurs of disbelief as I leaned on the railing eyeballing my shot. I thought about resetting, but glanced at my mother who looked like she'd pass out if I didn't take my shot soon and decided to go for it. I inhaled slowly and held my breath. I closed one eye. Too slow, and they'll celebrate without me. Just right... and I'd enjoy half a cruise before the temporal guardians blinked me back. The cool electronic cue slid back between my thumb and forefinger and paused before sliding forward to kiss the virtual ball, just right.

Half the room erupted with cheers and the other half groaned. A cluster of well-wishers patted and shook my arms as I descended the steps. My father stood at the bottom blocking my way. I paused on the last step so I was eye to eye with him and leaned my cue against the railing. My fingers seemed to have a mind of their own as they pulled the silver band from my right ring finger.

"Well played, Ginger," my father said and offered his hand as my mother appeared by his side.

I took his hand and nodded my thanks, but when I went to pull my hand away, he held on to it. His eyes narrowed, examining my face.

"Someday when I have a daughter, I'll name her Ginger after you," he said with a big grin.

I swallowed hard, unsure if I was causing massive time waves instead of little ripples, and then said, "I'd like that. And here," I placed my mother's wedding band in his hand. "Give her this, from me."

———

S. M. Kraftchak spends most of her time with dragons, elves, and aliens, yet still enjoys sunrise on the beach, sunset in the mountains and portraying Elizabeth Tudor. She has three awesome daughters, two dogs, and one cat. Her husband is her best friend, harshest critic and most fervent supporter. Writing is her passion.

DRAGON SLAYER[8]

Melodie Starkey

We waited down by the tracks until dusk, hunting for spikes and chewing wild spearmint and throwing rocks into the scrubby sagebrush across the irrigation canal, cheering when we roused a scurrying rodent or sometimes even a bird. Just before we heard it, we all felt it coming. We exchanged knowing glances without words, and strained to catch the first glimpse of it muscling toward us. The whistle sounded three sharp blasts as it entered the city limits, filling our ears and stomachs with anticipation. We spread out along the track where the levee was lowest and watched.

There is nothing and yet everything special about the car you finally choose: the door seems just a little further open or the handle shines just a little brighter or maybe the color is lucky for you. In the same instant you recognize it as the one, you are in motion, forward and up, your feet leaving the ground as your fingers contact the cold metal of the hand grip. You throw your body back first–away from the wheels– then up, catching the floor with your legs. And then you lie there, unable to move, unable to draw air into

---

[8] "Dragon Slayer" appears in Melodie Starkey's anthology, *Maybe It Was a Thursday* , 2010.

your terror-paralyzed lungs, until finally you gasp in that first painful breath and realize you are still alive. You gasp in your second breath, and let it out in laughter, rolling away from the opening to the dark, dusty safety of the car. You ache from your fingertips to your ribcage from the strain of holding on, but it's a good kind of hurting, and hugging yourself tightly eventually eases it.

We only rode two miles–into town. It wasn't the ride that mattered; it was the jump. When the train screamed down to a stop by the warehouses, we bailed out and ran into the shadows, meeting behind the Welch's grape juice bottling factory, each of us secretly counting heads to see if everyone had made it once again.

There were seven of us that summer of 1965, spending our long days haunting the vacant stretch of tumbleweeds and sagebrush between the tracks and the canal in our dusty little eastern Washington town. We were young enough that puberty hadn't segregated our play and tainted our friendships yet. I was one of three girls in the group, and about in the middle by age, so nothing made me special, except Jude.

Jude was always there, just on the outskirts of our games, sometimes standing in one place for hours at a time, watching our every move as if trying to decipher what type of creatures we were, at other times involved in fantasies of his own, waving a large stick in the air as if fighting off the occasional clouds that chanced by, or sitting on the tracks, carving pictures into the splintery black wood of the ties. We didn't worry about him sitting there because he certainly could tell when a train was coming in plenty of time to move.

Sometimes, out of a sudden sense of guilt-inspired duty, I'd say to the others, "Let's let my brother play, too." We'd all look over at him reluctantly, and if he was watching us he would smile. We'd wave him over, and I would try to show him what we were doing while he'd stand there grinning apishly, his eyes drifting around the group until I would punch his shoulder to get his attention back on me.

Jude didn't jump the trains. He would stand back and watch curiously as we all made our leaps, then he would walk home to wait for me on the back porch. Still, the trains fascinated him as much as they did the rest of us. With a red crayon he drew engines on every piece of paper he came across, and once on the living room wall, which earned him a sound whipping with the razor strop that was usually reserved for me.

One day we discovered an old wooden extension ladder buried in the weeds near the barbwire fence that marked the railroad easement and snagged our clothes when we wormed under it. The ladder was missing a few rungs, but still fairly sturdy. We dragged it over the tracks and down to the canal. It spanned the eight foot width of the canal with ease. Now nothing stood between us and the unconquered territory of the river bank!

Not trusting the remaining rungs, we crossed the ladder by walking with a foot on each of the stiles. It was shaky business, but the others got across safely, so I couldn't hesitate when my turn arrived. I was about half way across, trying to look only ahead and to remember just how deep the canal was, when one of those in front of me shouted, "Not Jude! Stop him!" I looked over my shoulder to see him, smiling away, stepping onto the ladder behind me. I shook my head and waved him back, but he just kept smiling and coming toward me. Finally I twisted around and shoved him. I saw him sit down hard on the bank just before I hit the water.

More surprising than the cold was the swiftness of the current. By the time I fought my head above water, the ladder was just a spanning twig far away from where I was. The water was so murky I couldn't see beneath the surface, so I twisted wildly, looking for anything to get hold of, my mind filling with memories of the eels that would sometimes get stuck in the backyard water spigots that were fed by this canal. I knew also that the canal went underground at some point to pass under the tracks and the highway–where did it surface again, if at all?

Finally I caught hold of the roots of a willow tree that were hanging over the canal bank like siphon hoses. I just held on, too frightened to do anything else, until the others arrived and pulled me out. My legs were trembling and I needed to vomit, but I managed to smile at them and comment, "Thought I'd go for a quick swim." I'd never admit how scared I was, just like we never discussed the terror of the trains, only the excitement. As we trudged along the bank to the ladder to get back across, the others assured me that they knew I was a goner and was going to get sucked into the pumps. Fortunately I had forgotten about the pumps–that was where the canal terminated: in huge, deafening pumps that shot the water out into a network of pipes which carried it to the surrounding farms and neighborhoods. If I had remembered, I probably would have been panic-stricken.

We suddenly heard a hideous noise, like a goose being strangled. Realizing it was just Jude, sitting on the opposite bank with his face against his raised knees, didn't make it any easier to listen to.

"Lucky he don't have to hear himself," someone muttered as we started crossing back.

I knelt beside him and turned his face toward me. When he saw that I was all right, he flung himself at me, burying his face against my wet shirt. The others stood around us, shuffling embarrassment, until I stood up, pulling Jude to his feet, and mumbled, "We better go home."

Mother's gaze slid right past my silty, wet clothes, lighting on Jude's tear-distorted face. She rushed over and hugged him against her, demanding, "What happened to him?" in a tone that made it clear that it was my fault, whatever it was.

"Nothing happened to him. I fell in the ditch. He got scared."

She frowned at my clothes then, and said, "What

ditch? You mean the canal? I've told you a thousand times to stay away from that canal! Get those clothes off and get in the bath this instant! That canal is full of diseases! Do you want polio? Do you want influenza? Where is your head?" Diseases were a big deal to her, because the doctor said Jude was the way he was from her having measles when she was pregnant. We weren't even allowed to have a dog because she knew they carried diseases.

***

I woke that night from a drowning dream, and crawled out of bed to stand by the open window until the sweat dried on my skin. Nothing stirred outside except a few suicidal moths throwing themselves against the porch lights. Suddenly the quiet was broken by the long, low whistle of the midnight freight. I smiled at the comforting sound and went back to bed.

I was grounded for a week. I sat in the kitchen teaching myself how to play the spoons until Mother threatened to use a wooden one on me if I didn't stop. I wandered from room to room pressing my face against windows, thinking about how the others were probably discovering all kinds of treasures along the riverbank. I lay on the couch and watched Jude sitting at the coffee table, happily filling his Big Chief tablet with red crayon drawings of trains. Gradually the drawings began to metamorphose into something new. They developed snouts, then wings, then fangs, and then fire coming out their nostrils and eyes with pupils like an angry cat's. He smiled satisfaction as he finished each new drawing and turned to start another. I wondered if I ought to mention it to one of our parents, but I figured I'd probably get in trouble for it somehow.

Finally, my confinement was over. Right after breakfast I headed out, hoping Jude would be content to stay home, but he caught up with me before I even reached the road. I sighed resignation and patted his shoulder, hoping the others wouldn't mind him coming along, because I doubted he'd stay put if we all crossed the canal without him again. I spotted the others sitting on the tracks, and jogged over to see what was up. Turned out the ladder had disappeared the first night, so they hadn't been exploring without me after all. They were now in the planning stages of trying to find enough scrap lumber that our dads wouldn't miss so we could build a fort. Sid volunteered that he could bring a large piece of tin for the roof, and maybe some nails. I wondered if the old man who lived behind us might have something in his shed I could pilfer. My own dad was an English teacher and could barely work a screwdriver. He was a complete embarrassment to have around when the car got a flat tire.

I glanced over a couple times to check on Jude. He was definitely glad to be out of the house again, too. He had located his favorite large willow branch and was waving it around like a conductor's wand then jabbing at the air with it, occasionally making cackling noises like a gagging parrot which we all recognized as his laughter. The tracks started their telltale vibration. We moved off of them languidly, silently agreeing the day was too hot to bother with trying to make the jump. As the engine chugged into view we dropped lazily to the ground several yards away, immune to the hot sand.

But something was wrong. Instead of the obligatory three sharp blasts from the whistle, the noise was constant and shattering, clenching our guts as we clapped our hands to our ears and leapt to our feet. And then the scream of the whistle was accompanied by the ripping shriek of the brakes as the engineer tried vainly to bring the hundreds of tons of mass to an instant stop. We all wheeled around, too late to do anything except watch as Jude held his stance in the center of the track, staff held high, challenging the beast.

***

None of us were allowed to play near the tracks again, even if we had wanted to. I can't hear a train whistle anymore without getting a chill down my back. Sometimes even now I get out his last tablet, which I hid from my parents during all the chaos following, and I study those drawings. What had he been thinking? What had he ever been thinking?

<hr>

Melodie Starkey's short stories have appeared in several literary magazines. Her novels are available on Amazon. You are invited to follow her on Facebook at: www.facebook.com/pages/Sunflowers-by-Melodie-Starkey/360781444004205?ref=hl

THE LAST WAVE GOOD-BYE[9]

Marjorie Rommel

Alec O'Donnell was a short, stubby Ulsterman of indeterminate years. His legs were slightly bowed, he wore a shock of thick black hair under his flat tweed cap, and on his tongue a brogue thick as shoe soles.

My grandfather Harry was a tall, skinny Englishman not long out of the Cheddar Hills of Somerset. His huge, knotted milker's hands hung below the rolled sleeves of his blue chambray shirts, his English upper lip covered a drawling Somerset accent – his name was "Hawry," he said – and under his gray fedora was a haircut regularly committed with a bowl.

Most evenings, the two men sat together on my grandparents' front porch till the sun went down and the coyotes started to yip in the woodlot back of the house across the road. They were talking of course – always talking – sometimes so intently they couldn't interrupt even to say goodnight.

Eventually, heads down, hands shoved deep in their overall pockets, they strolled down the long

[9] "The Last Wave Good-Bye" originally appeared as "The Last Long Wave Good-Bye" in *A Cup of Comfort for Inspiration: Uplifting stories that will brighten your day*, Colleen Sell, editor, © 2003 by Adams Media Corporation, 57 Littlefield Street, Avon MA 02322.

tree-lined drive, cut across the pasture past the swamp and through the gate into Alec's yard, where they stood talking another hour or so in the yellow cone of the high barn light – then they'd stroll back again. Some nights they made the trip three or four times before parting company.

Back on his own porch, each man would turn and wave to the other – one of those high, open-handed long-distance waves a man gives only, trustingly, to his favorite brother. Then each would go into his own house, blink the kitchen light, and retire to bed.

On a fine summer morning the year I turned eight, Grandfather took me with him to pay a call at O'Donnell's house. It was early, no one else awake, and the dew was thick as fairy gems spilled on the grass. My bare feet trotting to keep up with Grandfather's big booted ones, we walked down the lane, across the pasture, and through the gate at the foot of O'Donnell's orchard.

"Hello the house," Grandfather called, and the barn door flew open.

Alec O'Donnell stood there in his barn boots, his battered tweed cap jammed down around his ears. "Harry!" he called back joyfully, as if it had been years. "Ye coom visitin'!"

After a tour round the yard and barn, Alec led the way through his back door into the kitchen, a bare wood room occupied by a black cookstove, a plank table, two mismatched wooden chairs, and an up-ended coal scuttle.

I have no way of reckoning how long a time went by as I sat in privileged company with those men, listening to their talk, slurping strong hot tea from my saucer, eating fresh-baked brown bread slathered with new butter, dipping strawberries in brown sugar and Devon cream, but the sun went round from the east window to the south before Grandfather and I walked home.

Intense friendships – even those less enriched by proximity and goodwill, and less challenged by extremes of politics and temper and religion – are not easy to maintain. There were worms, I suppose, even in the good brown earth of Paradise. For my grandfather and his bosom friend Alec O'Donnell, that summer morning may have been the last of the good times.

Alec was, no doubt, a peculiar man. An Irishman living alone by choice, he never really left 'the ould sod,' and spent a great deal of time writing and reading letters from 'home.' I remember my parents discussing with astonishment this long, fast friendship between a ranging Ulsterman and an Englishman fiercely loyal to the queen.

The O'Donnell place was pretty, the neighbors allowed, but not in any kind of tidy, white-fenced American farm kind of way. Alec had built his small unpainted shake house on a slight rise at the foot of a hillside cherry orchard which every spring bloomed cloud white, sheep white, against the vivid grass and the piercing sky.

To the north was Grandfather's orchard, his clean dry pasture and splendid new red barn; to the west, the Olympic Mountains glowed in the setting sun; to the south, Mount Rainier's huge presence reigned. Cattails, blue and yellow flags, bog lilies, skunk cabbage and willow filled the marshy ground between Alec's little house and the road, screening the Irishman's domain from passersby. A gracefully curved thick willow branch grew horizontal to the ground, forming a natural settee – willow being the only thing that bog was good to grow, other than mosquitoes, my grandfather said. The willow settee stood leafy, rooted, and inviting at the water's edge.

Alec was considered something of a failure in our little immigrant farming community. He kept a few chickens, a pig, half a dozen milk cows. The animals kept him, but made little profit. There was a bull, too, at O'Donnell's – a glossy black angus as compact and well-muscled as its master – a bull we kids enjoyed baiting to draw it away from the Irishman's weedy orchard. Because of that bull, O'Donnell's apples were irresistible, and more than once we barely escaped the impact of its short gleaming horns ramming into the red board fence.

Aside from its periodic duties with Alec's cows and Grandfather's heifers, the bull had little to do. Our efforts to outwit him, we told each other, were by way of benevolent exercise, though Alec did not agree. When the fence fell to the bull's repeated assaults, we were required to replace it, a job Grandfather supervised, muttering under his breath.

Grandfather tried for years to convince his neighbor to get rid of the bull, which he considered dangerous, ill-tempered, and unnecessary. He also urged Alec to give up digging ditches by hand, and to drain the swamp instead – but his suggestions only made the Irishman angry.

How else if not with ditches, Alec demanded, was he to drain his fields and make them usable? Without his bog he'd be even more homesick. The bull, it seemed, was far more to Alec than just a way of getting a little cash by servicing the neighborhood cows. The beast was necessary to Alec's Northern Irish pride in some way only a bone-headed, stone-hearted Englishman could fail to understand.

When Alec fell ill in the fall of 1965 and the apples in his orchard fermented on the ground instead of elsewhere, the bull became quite inebriated. It broke through the fence, got mired in the bog, and lay there all night bellowing like Judgment till Grandfather came with his nightshirt tucked into his bib overalls and winched it out with a hand block and tackle.

But Alec felt sure, in the depths of his impetuous and decidedly less than logical Irish soul, that Grandfather's rescue had been the near death of his prize bull, rather than its savior. The argument that ensued was both vicious and sad.

"Ye gully!" O'Donnell roared.

Grandfather took his hands off the block and stood, propping his stiff back with his hands. "You're an ungrateful man, Alec O'Donnell," he said. Jerking his head at me to come away, he walked up the hill toward home, leaving Alec to hop and rage like an angry leprechaun, shouting Gaelic curses at our departing backs.

***

Thanksgiving came, then Christmas, but Alec's merry presence did not grace our holidays.

In spring, Grandfather made his annual trip to the Feed and Seed, where men of the area gathered to choose, sharpen, and rehandle their garden implements. Grandfather joined them, talking quietly, testing shovels and rakes for balance and heft, ringing choice hoes against the feed barn's cool cement floor.

The subject of their conversation, as it had been increasingly of late, was Alec O'Donnell and his sad fortunes, which the men feared might spread. Alec had been first in the community to come down with a new strain of Spanish influenza. Recalling the epidemic of 1918 that had killed so many, the neighbors were frightened. "It's that swamp," Krause said, sticking out his famous iron chin. "We should drain it for him, if he won't."

Such talk was not new, and I left them, but did not miss O'Donnell's entrance – or my grandfather's sudden stiff-necked posture. "Come away now," he said quietly, and motioned me out the door. Reluctantly, I followed him.

Alec recovered, but never regained his former strength and good humor. Nor did he and my grandfather resume their old friendship. That, I knew, had more to do with the wounded bull than with the devastation brought by flu.

By Christmas of 1966, the virus had swept through our community like fire in a stubbled field and then stormed away to cause grief in some other place. It wasn't much of a holiday, and once again, Alec O'Donnell was missing from my grandparents' table. The new year too, came and went – no puckish Alec with his fiddle to first-foot it, ducking and smiling, capering in through our back door and out the front to bring us luck. It was that, I think, that caused my grandmother to urge a truce.

"It's almost the new year, Harry. We've come through it all right, now let bygones be bygones." She stood on tiptoe to plant a kiss on Grandfather's weathered cheek, and I was suddenly aware that my round red-headed little granny must once have been very pretty indeed.

"Go now," she urged him, patting his shoulder. "There are twelve days to Christmas and they're not yet all gone. Friendship's a gift that won't dent your pocketbook." So Grandfather took up his hat and went.

I watched him trace the familiar path across the field, past the swamp, where he hesitated for one mighty long moment, then up through the orchard, straight to Alec O'Donnell's door – and right back again. "Slammed the door in my face," he railed at Grandma Kate. "I'm damned if I'll ever speak to him again."

Still, when Alec's health failed him again the following spring, Grandfather set aside the enmity between them. He took his old friend on the half–day drive to town, first to the doctor, then the hospital. He grumbled about neglected farm work and wasted time, but he visited Alec there every week, and months later he bore him home again, stubble-faced, pale, and scrawny.

Grandfather installed Alec in his own sagging bed in his own dusty front parlor and walked over several times a day––always going formally, the long way round by the road––to make sure the sick man's needs were met. It was clear, each time I went along, that they did not speak––at least not directly.

"Tell the old coot he needn't stir his bones, I can do for meself," O'Donnell crabbed at me.

"You're bull-headed as ever," Grandfather retorted, slamming down a mug of tea just far enough away so the sick man would have to reach.

Years later, long after I was grown and Alec O'Donnell had been reduced from his lowland farm to one of four beds in a nursing home ward, I dropped by on my lunch hour to bring him a stack of *Ireland Today* magazines and a sheaf of blue and yellow bog iris – and found Grandfather there. He had draped his cantankerous neighbor in an extra sheet, cranked him up in his bed, and was shaving him with the straight razor Alec once kept on the shelf in his tidy bachelor kitchen.

Making the same soothing throat noises he used to quiet his beasts, Grandfather applied hot towels to

Alec's sad and angry face. He brushed on thick lather, stropped the razor and applied it skillfully, maneuvering around the large, yet somehow delicate elfin ears, across wrinkles deep as drainage ditches, under the bagged eyes and sagging chin.

Three other old men watched intently, one standing by the window in a hospital gown and paper slippers, two others peering rheumy-eyed from under their covers. None noticed me, where I stood there in the doorway, thinking of the mired Black Angus bull. But then – it was a small moment, one I nearly missed – Alec O'Donnell, Irish to the soul, laid his weary head, deliberate and trusting, into my grandfather's gentle hold.

So I took my flowers and magazines, and went away tear-struck and smiling, remembering two huge hands raised in long greeting at twilight across an unproductive bog – and the kitchen light signal, a quicksilver message sent between two silent, distant stars.

———

Marjorie Rommel grew up in a small town, now a sizeable city, where she still lives. She was fortunate to spend part of her childhood in her grandparents' multi-national immigrant farming community. A newspaper reporter/editor for many years, she taught at Pacific Lutheran University, where she earned her MFA in 2007.

THE CLOSET MONSTER

Dixiane Hallaj

I pocketed my cell phone and pressed the up button on the elevator. The real estate agent was running late. Something about driving at a snail's pace behind a truck spreading salt. Never mind, this way I could poke around and take my time imagining the apartment furnished to my taste. She said a maintenance person had been in earlier and the door should be open.

"Hello, anyone here?" As I expected, there was no answer. I went in and started my tour. The view from the living room wasn't spectacular, but it beat the brick wall I'd faced for the last two years. The kitchen was perfect, compact and well designed. I moved on to the bedroom. My hand reached for the light switch to offset the early winter darkness and dropped before it got there. I didn't need more light. The room was an empty box; there was nothing to see.

I smiled to myself. My mother had ingrained frugality so deeply it must have become part of my DNA. I saw a sliver of light in the crack beneath the closet door and almost laughed. Mother had always been so worried that I would leave a closet light on that she had told me it would wake the closet monster if I did. I still couldn't quite forgive her for making me live with that fear, and many others, like the spiders that would come down and eat the dirt off my face if I didn't wash well enough before going to bed at night. I'd been so frightened that I avoided turning on the closet light at all. I'd even gone to school with mismatched shoes a few times because I pulled out the first shoes I found in the dark.

I took a deep breath, swallowed as many of those ridiculous fears as I could. Still nervous, I tiptoed across the room to turn off the light. No sense in disturbing the monster if he was awake. No switch on the wall, so there must be a pull chain inside. I opened the door.

I was staring right at the biggest belt buckle I'd ever seen — at eye level! The closet monster! Hidden from his terrible gaze by the low height of the doorframe, I did the worst thing I could have done, I screamed! I tried to turn and run, but my feet were rooted to the ground, paralyzed with fear. The loud crashing sounds of the monster breaking out of the closet echoed in the empty apartment. Everything went dark.

***

"Miss, are you all right?" The rough voice had a touch of Southern drawl that softened the edges.

"Miss Johnson, are you all right?" That was the realtor, Jane.

"Yes, I think so." My voice sounded weaker than I felt and I opened my eyes, only to blink several times in the light. I saw the outlines of two people kneeling next to me. I struggled to sit and a strong arm came around my shoulders to help me. "Thank you."

"What happened? Are you ill? Should I call someone?" Jane fired off questions faster than I could even start the answers.

"I guess we kind of startled each other." The man's understatement was cushioned in more than a hint of laughter. "I'd just fixed the light over the closet door when she opened the door and screamed like a real movie star." His laughter overwhelmed him and he had to stop for a minute. "My hand jerked and my electric screwdriver broke the light bulb. Don't exactly know what got me off balance, but the step stool went one way and I went the other." Still chuckling, he rubbed the back of his jeans.

"I wasn't expecting anyone. I called out when I came in, but I guess he didn't hear me." I finally got a good look at my closet monster. If I'd known he was going to be that handsome, I'd have left the lights on years ago.

––––––

Dixiane Hallaj lives in the small town of Purcellville, Virginia, with her husband of 53 years and their cat named Dog. She has four novels published by S & H Publishing, Inc. More about Dixiane at http://dixianehallaj.com *or* https://www.facebook.com/DixianeHallajAuthorPage?ref=hl

A CUP OF COFFEE

J. D. Kipfer

Jan got up every morning at five-thirty, brushed her teeth, put on her sweat clothes, grabbed her gym bag and headed for the YWCA swimming pool. Her mind was already busy with the arguments of the day to come and the unsatisfactory outcome of yesterday's debates. The stress of trying to make people realize that there was only so much money to go around – no one was going to get everything they wanted – had kept her tossing and turning most of the night. They were angry with her because she didn't get as much money from United Way, or DASA (Dept. of Substance Abuse), as she got the previous year. As a matter of fact, no one had come through with quite as much as last year.

Truth be told, they were angry at her because they were not going to get a raise. If she'd said: "You're all going to get a raise anyway," they'd have gone home happy.

She'd driven this back road so often she no longer noticed how beautiful the river was in wispy morning fog. Lost in her never ending arguments to justify herself, she didn't see the red-winged blackbird, balanced precariously on the top of a reed that grew along the river bank. She used to pull-over and watch for a while as the bird fluffed up his feathers and called out for a mate to come and join him. The mist above the river often gathered so low and dense he appeared to be on a cloud. Now, distracted by "pressures," Jan hardly noticed them anymore. Maybe distracting pressures were why some men were plotting to drain these fens and build luxury homes along the river; they just hadn't notice someone already lived there.

Suddenly aware that she had again whizzed by her favorite view, she promised herself she would notice next time. Damning God for making it such a beautiful day when she couldn't stay outside and enjoy it, surely he could have arranged a rain. She had been driving this same road at the same time for so long, that it seemed like the start of a dull regime in a long prison sentence. What did it matter what the day was doing, when you were locked away in an office, not doing anything to help the human race, not saving the planet, or writing a Pulitzer Prize novel, winning a Nobel Prize or even winning an Emmy Award.

Ah! Emmy Awards, her mind jumped the track to the TV she had watched the night before. What a relief it was to have something else, anything, just something other than drug addicts and drug counselors to think about — or were they the same people?

Her mind was like that, left alone to pursue its own path it wandered all over the place. Her mother was wont to complain that her body and her mind did not occupy the same universe. It was just as well, for unaided her body had reached the parking garage, ideally located between the 'Y' and her office. Reconnecting with herself, she considered what could have happened while her mind drifted. Somehow, she just didn't think a cop would find it much of an excuse if she said, "But officer, I was so busy thinking," when she broadsided someone in an intersection.

As always, she found a spot near the exit for a quick get-away at the end of the day. She grabbed her bag and sprinted to the 'Y.' After a few words of greeting with the lady at the desk, she hurried down to the lower level into the humid, chlorine-laden air, wafting up from the pool. She said a somnolent good morning to the other early morning swimmers. Some answered by a nod of the head, others just breathed a deep sigh, all of them, wishing they were going to jump back into bed instead of a swimming pool.

Jan stripped quickly, put on her bathing suit, tossed her things in a locker and jumped into the shower. She used to leave her shampoo in the shower so she wouldn't have to go into the locker room after her swim, until some ladies of the church, presumably after a night of prayer and reflection, used an entire bottle of her very expensive shampoo. They would have to pray for more; she wasn't going to contribute another bottle.

The water felt wonderful! Only swimming outside in a warm lake would have been better. While the guard was otherwise engaged, she broke the strict rules by swimming the first two laps underwater. She could no longer remember when she didn't swim, but water had become essential to her wellbeing. It was her sanctuary. She often took all of her troubles with her to the bottom of the pool and left them there. But she had no luck with that today. She was too upset by the injustice of those who tried to make her into a scapegoat for the weakness of the local economy. At least half of the funders that supported the agency had gone out of business, yet they insisted she had screwed up some way. They didn't know how she screwed up, but they certainly thought she had.

She only had time for twenty laps. Joe had called a meeting for the first thing this morning, and she wanted to have everything ready. Joe was the leader of their merry little band of mostly reformed drug addicts, who were now dedicated to helping others kick the habit. A motley crew if she ever saw one: There was Ed, a man so thin he looked like a walking question mark, creeping around the office, smoking one cigarette after another, a handkerchief always at the ready (a clear sign of cocaine abuse). Scott, the youngest of the crew, walked around looking like a fat Brad Pitt, constantly demanding that people mind their own business. He was dating Candy, a pretty blonde much older than he, who was also a counselor, although she strongly suspected Candy only counseled clients about easier ways to get a fix.

The rest of the crowd fit pretty much the same pattern except for Pat, who was the wife of an alcoholic. She was a woman who truly wanted to help women cope with their alcoholic husbands. When Jan had suggested divorce, Pat told her that was just running away, not solving the problem. Actually, Jan favored the well-planned murder, but she generally kept that to herself.

Then there was Diane, a short solidly built woman, who was the clinical director. She constantly had a narrow little cigar-like cigarette in her mouth. She was arrogant, and obviously felt superior to every one else. Maybe she had good cause. She'd been so possessed by alcohol when she was younger that she abandoned her husband and her two children. She fell to the very depths and was eventually hospitalized. Sober, she got a grip on her life, and now, with a BA and a Master's Degree in psychology, was the clinical director.

After the swim, Jan dashed to her locker, grabbed her shampoo, and took a quick shower. The gym bag had all that was necessary to turn her self-assessed ugly duck countenance into an aging swan, or at least a reasonable facsimile thereof, and she set to work.

Jan had left a very prestigious auditing firm to take this job in the hopes that it would offer her more variety, more interest, something to think about. She was aware that big firms tie their useful cogs to the same desk doing the same thing over and over again, especially if the cog happened to be a woman. As she twisted a hank of hair around her brush and applied the heat of the hair dryer, she imagined a beautiful office located in an equally beautiful location, and the pleasant experience of telling people that she worked there. Then she thought about the reality of her grubby room in the back of the office that had no windows – a place where the staff only came to complain. She resented the fact that people thought she, too, must have an alcohol problem because she worked there. Actually, she was the stable kingpin, writing all the copy for their literature, designing their brochures, going to Chicago for key meetings with DASA, and speaking at fund raisers up and down the river valley. It was better than just sitting in an office adding up figures all day. More and more now, she resented the feeling that she was slogging away doing all the real work for an office of dead beats. Even Diane was forty-five minutes late for a seminar she was holding on time management.

Now dressed for the day in her neat business suit, high heels and tasteful jewelry she looked every bit the full-fledged business woman. She always dressed smartly, ready for the unforeseen, no jeans and sweat shirts for her. She had to be ready for anyone who walked into the office be they banker, doctor, or policeman – or recovering alcoholic. While the motley crew was just that – motley.

A quick look at the clock and she realized that she was going to be late. It was her damn roving mind again; sometimes she wished she could turn it off, but, on rethinking, she decided that would mean being permanently dead.

Joe might be angry if she was late, or he might not, who could tell what Joe would do. He was head and shoulders over the rest of them academically, and she wondered just how long he would stay at the clinic after he got his PhD. He was a good looking Jewish boy; wore a full beard that he shaved off only once to reveal a lack of chin. Nevertheless, he was a very handsome young man. Joe had spent time in Israel in a kibbutz and was steeped in the history of his religion. Even though at Christmas, selling trees from the clinic's lot, he was the only one who knew the words to every Christmas carol extant. Obviously a brilliant man, he was almost childlike at times. At others, he was very authoritarian, the man in charge. But there were other times, like yesterday, when he was an absolute ass.

A quick trip to her car to deposit her gym bag, then down the hill and across the street and she was there. Inside the building, she waited impatiently for the elevator that would be reeking with the smell of whatever the janitor had used to cover up the deeply ingrained odors that had accumulated over the years. As the door opened, she put her hand over her mouth and held her breath. As often happened, she was slightly dizzy by the time she got to the fifth floor.

The front door of the office was still closed but she could hear Mary Ann's radio blasting the latest rock sensation from the other side. She liked music, but not other people's loudly imposed taste. Oh well, she steeled herself for the blast of noise, opened the door and saw her three-hundred pound receptionist dancing like a teen-ager across the office, singing to

A CUP OF COFFEE/KIPFER

the music of somebody called "Dr. John." Not a bad voice, either.

Jan walked over to the radio and turned the volume down, and in reply to Mary Ann's little pout said, "Only for a minute, please. I can't talk over that noise."

Mary Ann was one of life's great delights. She got her job through CETA, a government agency to find work for people with no, or low work skills. Well, she could type fairly well, and her filing system required a little imagination to find things, but she had an under-estimated skill that couldn't be taught – she could handle people. A beautiful face, surrounded by wild blond curls that never seemed to be combed, she reminded Jan of "Miss Piggy" of Muppet fame. Mary Ann only earned minimum wage, and she had a teenaged daughter to care for, yet she often shopped in second-hand stores for women's underwear to give to the agency for abused women.

After a bit of small talk and an exchange about the day's work load, Jan finally said, "Isn't Joe here yet?"

"No. He's always got places to go and people to see before he gets in," Mary Ann answered, arranging her desk for the day ahead.

"What's he doing? Running for office? He was going to have a staff meeting this morning."

"Mine not to reason why, mine but to be here and mind my own business," Mary Ann said, and motioned her head toward the office door, her hands full of mail. "Open that, will you?"

"Are any of the counselors here yet?" Jan asked, more than a little incredulous.

"Um, not exactly. Don't worry, I can handle anybody that comes in. You go on back to your office and don't worry about the clients. If Warren Buffet or Bill Gates comes in with a big check, I'll call you."

Jan stepped back across the office and opened the door. "If either one of those gentlemen calls, have them wait for Joe."

Leaving Mary Ann chortling at her desk, Jan went down the hall to her own office. She had plenty of work waiting for her. But she couldn't concentrate; her mind was too occupied with planning her strategy for Joe's meeting.

Halfway through the morning she became aware of angry voices coming from the front office. She hesitated going back to see what the problem was, but Mary Ann was up there all by herself and maybe someone, with a little more authority, could help.

She walked back down the hall, gratefully noticing that Mary Ann had made the coffee; she'd get a cup on the way back.

The first thing she noticed when she stepped into the front office was Mary Ann standing behind her desk, pale as a ghost, glaring at the front door, holding her staple gun in her hand like a weapon. Jan turned toward the door and froze. She felt hollow, like all the blood had been drained from her body. Mary Ann's staple gun wouldn't have helped a bit.

Standing in the doorway, his head only inches away from the lintel, was the biggest, man she had ever seen. He had his hands above his head, holding on to the trim above the door, letting his upper body lean into the room. The suit jacket he was wearing made his shoulders seem as wide as the door, but he wasn't fat. He was not only the biggest man she'd ever seen but damn near the most handsome. His nose was long and narrow and his cheekbones were almost to his eyebrows. He looked like he was carved of stone – a big black, ebony stone. His skin actually glistened, and the whites of his eyes were even whited because of the contrast.

When he smiled his mouth stretched across his face revealing teeth as white as his skin was black. And he was smiling at her with that malevolent expression on his face of a cat ready to pounce on a mouse that has nowhere to go.

"He wants coffee. Joe left strict orders that I wasn't supposed to give him anymore," Mary Ann said from the protection of her desk.

His name was Voice, and he was a notorious drug abuser. Jan had never seen him, but she'd heard enough about him to know that she and Mary Ann were in real peril. Mary Ann had been giving him coffee to keep him calm when she was here alone. Unfortunately, Joe had gotten off the elevator one morning just as Voice was getting on with a cup of coffee from the office.

Voice had raised his cup in greeting and said, "Thanks for the coffee, Joe."

Joe's anger had far exceeded Mary Ann's crime. He had shouted at Mary Ann that the coffee was for clients. if Voice wanted the privilege, he must come in for counseling – if she didn't agree with him, she could go work somewhere else.

Joe was rarely around to help with difficulties early in the morning, yet he insisted that Mary Ann open the front door promptly at eight.

In the fleeting seconds of standing there, a lot went through Jan's mind. "Dammit, Joe, where are you? Well, I'm here. I'll do this my way.

Mary Ann deserves better support. The rest come drifting in as it pleases them, but I'm here all day long and back in the evenings for meeting with the funders. They yell and fuss about who's got the money, but whose minding the clients?"

She turned and looked at Voice, and wondered if the crowd trying to save the river fens needed a fund raiser.

Then she looked the giant in the eye, smiled and said, "How do you like your coffee, Voice?"

Jean (J.D) Kipfer was born in Southern West Virginia. She left WV to go to Dayton, Ohio where she studied at the Dayton Art Institute. While she raised her son, she began to write. Her latest novel, Indian Blood, is part of S & H Publishing's catalogue. Jean lives in Zebulon, NC where she writes stories and paints pictures.

OUT OF THE BOX

Wendy Wong

Jonathan Laidlaw placed the cardboard box onto his desk and sighed. This was it. The summation of his life for the last 41 years - about to be tossed into a 12 x 18 inch cardboard box.

This sure as hell wasn't his idea. When the company had offered him an early retirement package four years ago, Jonathan had turned them down point blank. Now they'd taken the offer off the table and simply handed him a pink slip. Jonathan was being "downsized". He'd been handed a cheque for the exact amount of severance due, along with a ticket to an all-inclusive golf resort in South Carolina - *in appreciation of his years of dedication and service*.

Hah! Jonathan didn't even play golf. Bayou Glen Resort was owned by one of the agency's biggest clients and management had gotten a good deal on the package. *Why couldn't they have just given him a gold watch?*

He picked up the framed photograph of his trophy wife/former secretary, Mindy. It had been on his desk for the last seven years but he'd never really had time to examine it closely. Without question, Mindy was a beautiful woman – from the tips of her gloriously highlighted hair to her cherry red pedicured toes. These days, Jonathan didn't doubt for a minute that luscious Mindy was more attracted to his executive salary than his sixty-two year old body with its spare-tire and comb-over. Once it had become obvious that Jonathan's career would never reach beyond middle management, Mindy's affections had cooled. For the last two years, she'd been having an affair with her current boss and before that, there had been the stockbroker. Jonathan had discovered his wife's infidelity quite by accident one morning when he'd inadvertently mistaken her cell phone for his own. Upon checking the inbox, he'd found some very lurid sext messages - complete with photos revealing parts of Mindy that Jonathan hadn't seen in years. Sooner or later he'd have to deal with it but somehow, it just didn't seem all that important.

From the bottom left-hand drawer Jonathan pulled out another photograph. This was the wife that counted. Slightly overweight – Mary had never lost those extra pounds after giving birth to their son, JJ. Jonathan smiled when as he looked down at her pleasant but forgettable face. They'd been married right out of university and had lived in a tiny hovel of an apartment while she'd supported him through grad school. Eventually they'd scrimped and saved enough to buy a bungalow in the suburbs and start a family. Then, just when his career was taking off, Jonathan had traded in the Volvo for a BMW and had left Mary for Mindy. *What had he been thinking!*

Mary had died of breast cancer two years later and
JJ hadn't spoken to his father since. Jonathan
carefully put Mary's photograph into the box -
placing the two wives back-to-back so they wouldn't
have to look at each other. Then he added his
"World's Greatest Dad" coffee mug.

Outside his office door the company's Boy
Wonder was stacking his boxes, waiting to move into
Jonathan's space. The vultures had been scrapping
over his coveted corner office ever since word of
Jonathan's "retirement" had reached the coffee room.
Every company has their share of Boy Wonders –
career zealots with an uncanny knack for being in the
right place at the right time. They schmoozed their
way up the ladder by golf buddy connections and
strategic social climbing. Jonathan had been there
and done that. Eventually, Boy Wonder would burn
one too many bridges and find himself wedged up
under the glass ceiling with a lot of vengeful co-
workers celebrating his demise. That is - unless he
was one of those people who'd been born with a
horseshoe up his ass. If that was the case, then Boy
Wonder would one day become a partner with his
name on the door.

Jonathan turned and faced his ego wall and then
began taking down the awards and diplomas,
leaving rectangular patches of un-faded paint.

Now the certificates were yellowed with age - the
most recent dating back to 1981. In his day, Jonathan
had been "The Boy Wonder" at Birch Marketing.
He'd been the company's secret weapon - winning all

kinds of accolades and promotions for his award winning campaigns. Jonathan's old-school clients had been fiercely loyal to him. Back then, all it took were a few baseball playoff tickets and plenty of liquid lunches – combined with the occasional all-nighter to meet a deadline.

One by one, the old boys had retired and a new breed of client had moved into the biz. They didn't "do" lunches. Some of them were women who used their lunch hours to buy groceries or shop for their kids. How the hell was he supposed to talk guy stuff with someone who had to co-ordinate their schedules with day-care and P.T.A. meetings?

Jonathan picked up his stapler and dropped it into the box. It really didn't belong to him but he'd used that same damn stapler for the last 30 years and he wasn't about to give it back. Then he added his Rolodex. Nobody would want that. All of the new account service people used computers to keep track of their contacts. They could access client birthdays and supplier phone numbers with a tap on their iphones. And they could delete them just as easily. Jonathan's Rolodex was crammed full of people he'd met and many who he hadn't contacted in years. Some had even died, leaving their names immortalized in the circle of the Rolodex.

Tossing the magnetic paper clip holder in after the Rolodex Jonathan shrugged pragmatically. Change was inevitable and no one knew this better than Jonathan Laidlaw. Over the years, he'd witnessed plenty of change. The receptionists had been replaced with voice-mail, the paste-up artists with Mac Operators, the typewriters with desktops and plain speech - with politically correct platitudes.

He gazed out the window at the office directly across from his in the tower next door. Ten stories up was Jonathan's parallel universe. While the occupants had been replaced over and over again, they all looked just like Jonathan – same off-the-rack suit, same Father's Day tie and the same stack of papers piled high on their desk. He'd watched their tantrums, witnessed their gloom as they'd filled their own boxes. And still Jonathan had stayed on.

The company had changed over time. It was no longer the powerhouse it had once been. Under the recently new leadership of Birch Junior, a downward slide had begun. The founder's son was one of those kids who'd been handed everything in life and didn't know what to do with any of it. The most prestigious private schools had been unable to provide Junior with two crucial things every businessman needs to survive – something money just couldn't buy – a hunger for success and basic gut instincts. Hence was the need for Birch Marketing to re-evaluate its assets, examine potential cost cutting areas and thus "downsize" Jonathan Laidlaw -which led Jonathan to the last item for his box.

It was a card signed by all of his co-workers. They each wrote some quirky little message like - *You lucky dog*...or...*we'll miss you John Boy*...or... *Don't be a stranger*. One misguided signer had obviously been in a hurry when he'd signed *Happy Birthday Irena!*

SHORT & HAPPY (OR NOT)

With the card Jonathan's co-workers had included a gift card for Home Depot. Jonathan lived in a condo. Not once in his life had he ever wired a switch, sawed a board, laid a tile or installed a toilet. What the hell was he going to do with a $55 gift card for Home Depot?

He tossed the card into his box and dropped the box onto his office chair. The chair was his. Shortly after he'd begun "seeing" Mindy, Jonathan's back had started giving trouble. He'd contacted office services and had requested a chair with lumbar support. The office manager had curtly replied that he had a perfectly good chair and that there was no need for a replacement. So, Jonathan had bought his own chair with his own money. Then he'd gone to the supply cupboard and reimbursed himself with pens, printer paper, staples, ink cartridges – anything in a box that he could use to stock his home office. Now, he was bloody well taking his chair with him! He wheeled it out the door, down the hall and onto the elevator. The chair wasn't going to fit into his Volvo – *Mindy drove the Beamer* - but he damn well wasn't going to leave it at Birch Marketing.

Getting the wheelie through the revolving door and out onto the street was no easy feat but Jonathan was on a roll. Much to the consternation of the security guard, he wiggled and bumped his way out of the building. After slogging the chair backwards down the concrete front steps in front of the office tower, Jonathan found himself standing on the sidewalk looking back up at the building that had consumed his life for forty-one years.

Taking a deep breath, Johnathan forced himself to look away. His eyes panned the busy city square. Down the block, he spied a street person warming himself over a subway grate and knew he'd found a home for his top-of-the-line ergonomic five hundred twenty-eight dollar and fifty-three cent chair. He left it with the bum.

Next on his agenda, Jonathan scanned the area until he found what he was looking for. A garbage can – not the domed kind with the flap that bit your hand when you tried to put anything into it but one of those big, square, open mouth garbage receptacles that the city lined with green bags. Walking over to it, Jonathan rested his carton on the lip of the can. On second thought, he fished out the golf resort package and after a moment's further hesitation, the Home Depot gift card. *What the hell. You never know when you might need a sump pump.* And then Jonathan Laidlaw dropped the box with the wives...the awards ...the coffee mug from the son who hated him... and all the other pieces of his life that meant nothing... into the can.

———

Wendy Wong worked for seventeen years as a copywriter at one of Canada's largest advertising agencies, then went freelance when her daughters were born. Today she lives in Etobicoke, Ontario and writes children's books. She is currently working on her first novel. You can contact her at: www.wendybooks.ca

THE UNCERTAINTY PRINCIPLE

Maria Elizabeth McVoy

In 1927 a German theoretical physicist, named Werner Heisenberg, articulated that one could not simultaneously measure both the exact position and motion of a particle. By shining one quantum of light on the particle, to accurately determine its current position, one would disturb that particle and change its motion unpredictably. This principal is called the Uncertainty Principle.

Rowena closed her eyes and took a slow breath, inhaling through her nose and exhaling through her mouth. Then she turned the doorknob and entered the boardroom. This was the part of science that she distinctly disliked: begging for funding from government and private patrons. Experimentation was expensive, and as much as she hated requesting funds, she could hardly support this particular project out of her own bank account. So, here she was, facing a panel of directors from Tanto, a rapidly declining, and almost forgotten, video game label.

She handed out typed packets of her proposal, which the panel immediately began to leaf through mechanically. She waited for their response with an outward appearance of complete calm. An old man, with glasses so thick and filthy that she wondered if

THE UNCERTAINTY PRINCIPLE/McVOY

he could actually see through them, closed his packet and looked at her directly. "So, what exactly is it that you are proposing, doctor?" he inquired. His voice was like crisp leaves batting against one another in the breeze.

Her voice echoed clear to the stark, white corners of the room. "The objective of our study is to provide exposure therapy to thirty-nine phobic subjects, and, for the sake of control, thirty-nine non-phobic subjects. All of the participants in this study will be volunteers and will be compensated for the time they allot to this project. We will use specially engineered computer games to expose the subjects to phobogenic stimuli. The average person gets slight anxiety from spiders, from enclosed spaces for long periods of time, and from extreme heights. The virtual environment of the video games should produce mid-range levels of anxiety for the phobic subjects. These levels of anxiety should help to treat, and eventually to reduce, the phobia to a typical level of situational discomfort. We hope to prove that the video games we design together are the next gen tools for the treatment of phobias. That is our end-goal."

"An interesting proposal, doctor." he said, obviously intrigued.

"Thank you, sir." His interest almost surprised her. She had prepared herself for the very real possibility that her project would not even be taken seriously.

"And this sum," he glanced with obvious apprehension at the page in front of him.

"The sum I am requesting will cover the price of equipment, employee costs, and sundries — such as the compensation for the seventy-eight participants. We propose that our psychologists work hand-in-hand with your programmers and engineers to design the games. Quite frankly, we see this as a beneficial enterprise for both parties. If our experiments are successful, then a commercial product would be a realistic possibility."

He nodded in affirmation. "Then, gentlemen, before we sign this contract, are there any more questions?"

An even older gentleman beside the first responded in a voice deeper and louder than she would have expected: "Is there a possibility that this experimentation will have adverse effects on the subjects?"

Rowena raised her left eyebrow, as the old man responded: "Adverse effects from playing video games?" Muffled laughter flowed around the table like a leaf caught in a whirlpool.

***

Eight months later

The door to Rowena's office was always left open. It gave her full view of the hallway where she could witness the claustrophobia patients enter and exit the floor. She watched with disappointment as Subject 13 — Kyle, veered away from the elevator to take eighteen flights of stairs to the ground. Frustrated, she glanced at Kyle's data on the sheet in front of her.

It seemed only yesterday that she had appeared before the panel of directors for Tanto, and they had

175

signed a contract initiating the Arcadia-Tanto merger. They had three current projects, designed by psychologists, computer programmers, and engineers who jokingly referred to themselves as "Team Olympus:" The Daedelus project for the treatment of acrophobia, the Thesius project for the treatment of claustrophobia, and the Arachne project for the treatment of arachnophobia. So far the subjects were dealing admirably with their phobias in the virtual environment of the interactive suites. However, as she had just witnessed, they were hesitant to face their phobias outside of the game environment.

She took some hope from the fact that none of the participants, control or phobic, had actually made it through all the levels of any of the games. As with most video games, the levels got progressively harder. Since these particular games were designed to treat phobias, they also progressively got more frightening for the phobic patients. Rowena sighed. She would just have to wait patiently for the game to play itself out.

***

At intervals the walls were literally crawling with vines, as the seemingly conscious tendrils writhed and lashed out at anything that moved too suddenly. Sometimes they just lashed out at random when nothing was moving, perhaps a defect in the program. Kyle found himself sucked into the game; while he played he forgot himself, as his entire existence focused on solving the maze and accumulating points. Twelve points put one more second on the clock.

Kyle had gained a little room to breathe. He pressed the red button on his gauntlet to pause the game briefly, and then pressed the blue to illuminate his score on the spherical projection screen around him—

2043 points.

A little less than three minutes of playing time. The game began with fifteen minutes on the clock, and those first fifteen minutes were the most important for accruing points. If he didn't accrue enough in the first fifteen minutes, he was barely able to keep ahead of the clock. Hitting adversaries gained points, and being hit depleted them. But it was still the clock, not any physical enemy, that always beat him in the end.

Unpause.

Kyle aimed his crossbow accurately and shot away a vine high above him on the left that had started to jiggle a little too ominously—thirty-six more points.

He hesitated with his back against a bare wall and readied his crossbow before turning the corner. A sharp jolt hit his leg, then another. Goblins! The electric shocks that simulated bombardment had taken him off guard when he first played the game; he had since grown used to, and even enjoyed, the realism. He aimed down at the three-foot tall monsters and exacted two shots on each of their sparsely-haired heads.

120+120+120=360 points.

The corridors always seemed to grow narrower as he progressed through the maze. Vines receded from the walls to crawl along the ceiling. Goblins, in groups of three to eight, patrolled the dark corridors of the maze — sometimes crouching along the ground and other times swinging from the vines overhead. Often the last Goblin in a patrol would turn tail when he found himself alone and run to get reinforcements.

Kyle knew he was almost out of time. It had been a good game today, well over two hours of hard playing. The corridor around him was unfamiliar and, he hoped, fairly close to the final challenge in the center. Perhaps only half a dozen corridors lay between him and the Minotaur. Tomorrow, he was sure, he would accrue enough time to get there.

Suddenly the projection sphere around him flickered in and out, sending him into brief darkness. Kyle felt a lurch in his chest, a break in the steady rhythm of his heart. *What the...*he wondered. A hollow, and surprisingly chipper, text-to-speech synthesis drowned out the soundtrack of the game: "We are experiencing a malfunction in the program; please continue playing or press the red button on your control gauntlet to exit."

What the hell does that mean, 'malfunction in the program?' He looked at the walls around him, at the flawless graphics, which disguised the fact that he was standing on, under, and in the middle of a hollow projection sphere. What if the malfunction caused the computer to hang? What if the whole system short-circuited and the entire building experienced electrical failure? The building, he knew, was set up like many modern hotels, with card swipes to unlock the doors. Electrical failure would mean being trapped in this room. Kyle placed his hand over his chest, as if through physical pressure he could slow the violent thrashing of his heart. He punched the red button on his gauntlet frantically, but nothing happened. Was he trapped?

The happily detached voice came back, echoing through the empty corridor: "We are experiencing a malfunction in the program; please continue playing or press the red button on your control gauntlet to exit."

His brain felt as if it were in a clamp. If the malfunction prohibited him from pausing or stopping the game, might it not also prevent him from leaving if he lost? By the time he found out it would be too late to change. He had just one other option: to beat the entire game. He pressed the blue button to check his time —

00:01:30...00:01:29...00:01:28...

This was impossible.

No, it was a goddamn computer game. He rubbed his temples, trying to force the painful knots out of his brain. If he was ever going to beat this game, now was the time. And it was running out fast. Where were those little bastard goblins when he needed them?

Kyle broke into a jog, racing around two corners before he saw any movement. Yes! A patrol. He opened fire, killing three before they even had time to turn. Four others were disposed of quickly before they could place a hit on him. He couldn't afford to lose points to anything but time. The last goblin he allowed to race away down a side corridor. *Yes*, he thought, *go get your friends.*

He continued jogging; his breathing became ragged and painful. This had to be the right way: the corridors were definitely getting narrower. He knew if he tried he could easily touch his hands simultaneously to both walls. He tried not to focus on it, but fear crept into his mind as the walls grew closer and the ceiling came down to meet his head. He had to duck to shoot the vines now.

The music around him had increased its tempo, echoing his urgency and the rapid beat of his heart against his ribs. He had to be close now. He hadn't seen a patrol in a full two minutes, an unheard of lapse, in his experience.

He slowed his jog as his ears picked up a bass sound, under the music, which seemed to shake the ground beneath his feet. At the end of the corridor, he made a final abrupt left and entered the center — it had to be the center — of the labyrinth. The room was small, about the size of a large elevator — and it was already occupied. Sconces high on the walls licked flame against stone. Like oil on water, the black ceiling seemed to move and change color. Vines, he realized, the entire ceiling was made of vines. He hoped the fire would keep them from coming down. In the center of the room was a broken column on top of which was a red button, much like the one on his gauntlet, which could pause, stop, or, at the outset, start the game. And between the column and Kyle was the Minotaur, pacing like a caged creature, restless and hungry for exercise. It was seven feet tall, at least, and its horned bull's head nearly touched the vine ceiling as it reared up on its hind legs. The creature roared, making that sound, which vibrated through the near corridors of the labyrinth. Any minute now it would realize that its space had been invaded. And then all Hades would break loose.

Why wait?

Kyle aimed carefully and released a volley of bolts, catching the Minotaur full in the abdomen. Seven bolts punctured the creature's tender underbelly; it let forth a howl that almost knocked Kyle off his feet as it turned and lunged in his direction. Kyle jumped to the side — not quickly enough as his left arm went numb from the Minotaur's downward punch — shooting erratically, two bolts sunk into the ceiling earning him a few precious seconds, and a third sunk deep into the Minotaur's right eye. It was half blind now. That was all Kyle needed. He stood up in the monster's blind side and released another volley of bolts, ducking down behind the column without even seeing if his bolts had hit.

Time, how much time? He pressed the blue button — 120 points. Ten seconds.

He took a deep breath, slowly, in his nose and out his mouth, to calm his racing pulse. It was now or never, and he wasn't prepared to spend any longer in the labyrinth. Kyle stood up and maneuvered around, keeping the column between him and the bull's head. The creature still had the bolts stuck in its belly, but they hardly seemed to be slowing it down. Kyle knew he couldn't afford to be hit another time. He shifted his feet, keeping that column between them and opened fire, angling the bolts upwards into the creature's heart. Ignoring the onslaught, it lunged towards him across the column. It was over then: could this thing not be killed? Kyle kept firing, expecting any moment for his limbs to go numb from the creature's blows. But the Minotaur's right eye glazed over in death; it collapsed against the column, snapping bolts as its weight pressed down on the red button.

***

Rowena closed Kyle's file as an attendant escorted him into her office. She smiled congenially into his pallid features. "Congratulations. Your claustrophobia has improved dramatically over the past two months. With time, and a little more therapy, your anxiety should recede completely from phobic levels to more comfortable levels. Although you should not require any more sessions in the sphere, I would recommend that you consider using the alternative video game that Arcadia-Tanto now offers; we're forwarding you a redemption code to download the game on your device of choice."

He listened to the doctor without really hearing her. When she finished, he retreated to the hallway and pressed the red button to call the elevator. Once inside the narrow, metal box, he inhaled through his nose and exhaled slowly through his mouth. Abruptly, the elevator stopped on level three. As the sliding doors opened, Kyle raised his arm automatically to fend off an impending attack.

***

Rowena re-opened Kyle's file and glanced at the last memo she had received from the observation lab: "Theseus Subject 13, Kyle Dougherty, passed the Minotaur with induced malfunction — claustrophobia anxiety nominal."

She picked up the direct line to the Arachne Project — "Yes. Malfunction stimulus was used successfully in the Theseus Project. Initiate malfunction stimulus on Subject 37."

Maria Elizabeth McVoy enjoys solving mazes but, alas, does not actually play videogames of any variety. She is the author of "Thirteen Years of Christmas," and the co-author of two adorable children: Michael who was born on the Epiphany; and Rosina who was born on Mardi Gras.

THE WATER BOMB WAR

Marjorie Rommel

Our next-door neighbor Mrs. Goodlady felt perfectly justified in helping herself to the apples under *our* tree, in *our* yard, but had an absolute fit if we picked the half dozen or so marionberries that stuck through our fence from *her* yard every summer. More than once my sister Kate and I caught hell for what was clearly sheer injustice. We were flat-out *incensed*. And Kate was motivated to revenge.

Kate had a thing about water bombs. You know, the kind kids used to make out of paper sacks filled with water? We learned how to make and deploy them from the *Book of Knowledge Encyclopedia* we rescued from somebody's flooded basement, hauled home in our Red Flyer wagon, dried out in the woodshed, and bound together with rubber bands begged from the paper boy.

Very interesting, the 26 or so volumes of that encyclopedia – it taught us everything from belly dancing to finger spelling to well, making water bombs.

Imitating sensuous Arab ladies neither of us had ever seen, Kate could roll her stomach like nobody's business. We learned to sign M-E-R-R-Y-C-H-R-I-S-T-M-A-S to the man who sold pencils on the sidewalk outside Frederick & Nelson's – he was so excited he gave us each a yellow pencil, free! For weeks, we slaved away learning to read each others' mind. It didn't work. But the water bomb lesson, something we could get serious teeth into, really took.

Quickly grasping the potential for aerial surveillance and bombardiering, Kate experimented exhaustively, collecting good thick suitably-sized paper bags, carefully folding and reinforcing them, filling them with water – never more than half, lest they burst too soon – standing on the toilet seat in the upstairs bathroom and dropping them into the claw-footed tub.

Once she had payload and trajectory just right, she concentrated on perfecting her aim, releasing water bombs from our third-floor bedroom window straight down into the cinder driveway, occasionally drenching one of the neighborhood cats. She was truly dedicated to her cause: protecting our apples from unneighborly sneak attacks.

On this particular day she brought a jug of water and a paper bag up into the apple tree, out onto the wooden platform where I lay all innocent, mind, shaded in leaf-dapple, nibbling oatmeal-raisin cookies and reading *Great Expectations*.

We'd been up there all morning, Kate and I, peaceful as Sunday, when Old Mrs. Goodlady came marching over with her bucket, which she filled with our apples, without so much as a by your leave. Leaned over like that, her backside looked – from above – remarkably like the hind end of one of our grandfather's Guernsey cows. And right there on her lower back, just above her haunches, a nice flat landing pad cried out for a sack of *something* to be dropped on it.

"Sarah!" Kate hissed. "Help me!" I went on reading, holding her skirt in one fist as anchor as she leaned far over the platform edge, paper bag poised. The platform swayed with the rustle of leaves and brown paper, followed by a satisfying "smack!"

Gramma Goodlady, as we were supposed to call her, issued an unladylike whoop, dropped her bucket, and big juicy gravensteins rolled every which way. She stormed out of our yard, yowling as if she'd been shot. Kate and I laughed till we cried.

The subsequent uproar didn't stop Mrs. Goodlady from rustling our apples. Didn't stop us from defending said apples, either. Yes, we got in trouble, though not as much as we expected.

And the war went on.

———

Marjorie Rommel grew up in a small town, now a sizeable city, where she still lives. She was fortunate to spend part of her childhood in her grandparents' multi-national immigrant farming community. A newspaper reporter/editor for many years, she taught at Pacific Lutheran University, where she earned her MFA in 2007.

LEFT BEHIND

Colleen Grimes

I watched my mother leave in a small white bus, as it pulled from the curb and headed for the asylum. Two men helped her to the bus, as she looked straight ahead, expressionless, not looking at me or my father. I ran into the street and began waving, as the bus disappeared from view.

My father gently took my hand and squeezed it, telling me my mother was sick and was to be gone for awhile. Even at eight years old, I knew something was wrong, but I didn't understand. Sometimes I could hear her crying at night, when she thought I was sleeping, and my father always looked tired and worn out when he fixed my supper.

That night as he tucked me in, he told me that I was to live with another family for the summer. They were an Amish family with a farm not far away. He told me that there would be lots of adventures and children to play with, and he would visit me on the weekends. I quietly listened, as he pulled the covers over me and kissed my forehead. I already missed my mother, and wondered when I would see her again.

We got up early and had breakfast together. The house seemed empty without her, but my father did his best to keep things normal. He even made pancakes, with fresh blueberries, a meal reserved for special occasions.

Father helped me pack my suitcase, we ran a few errands in town, and then set out for the Indiana countryside. Leaving the city behind, we drove through lush, amber fields of wheat and corn, grazing cattle, and magnificent horses shading themselves under weeping willow trees. After driving for over an hour, the main road ended and we found ourselves on a dusty one-lane gravel road winding through a large grove of trees.

The road abruptly ended and looming before us was a large, clapboard house, plain, with no shutters or curtains in the windows. There was no grass to speak of, only dirt. When we got out of the car, chickens were running around the yard, clucking about our feet. I clung to my father, as he took my hand to reassure me.

The screen door to the porch opened and a lady with a dark blue bonnet and white apron came down the steps to greet us. She wore no smile on her crinkled face, but it appeared kind, just the same.

Looking up into a window on the second floor, I saw many children huddled around it, trying to get a better look at the strangers who had come to visit. I soon learned there were nine children in the family — six boys and three girls.

From a distance, I saw a horse coming up the drive. A tall, lanky man got off the horse and walked over to us. He wore bib overalls and had a long beard. He greeted me with a broad smile and a warm handshake. I liked him right away. Now, I had officially met the Yoder family. My father was asked to stay for supper, but he chose to leave, as he had a long drive home.

Just as I had watched my mother leave only a day before, I watched his car slowly drive down the dusty driveway and disappear from sight.

Mrs. Yoder put her hand on my shoulder, took my hand and led me into their home. The kitchen was sparsely furnished, with an icebox, a wood-burning stove, an open cupboard and a huge wooden table set with a lace tablecloth. There were twelve mismatched chairs around it. I was happy they had provided one for me. The children scurried down the stairs and into the kitchen to take a better look at me. I managed a weak smile, as the girls giggled and the boys stared at me in curiosity.

We all sat down and were instructed to bow our heads, as a brief prayer was said by their father. I was unaccustomed to this ritual, but it felt good and I was thankful.

I had never before seen so much food at one time. There were two roasted chickens with boiled potatoes, snap peas, summer squash and homemade biscuits. A large pitcher of cold milk sat on the table. Two fresh apple pies dusted with cinnamon sat on the cupboard, waiting to be served. I hungrily ate all that was on my plate, patiently waiting for dessert. The apples were both sweet and tart at the same time, and I savored each and every bite.

The girls were responsible for cleaning up after meals, as the boys went outside to finish their chores. Elizabeth, sixteen and the oldest, led me outside with two pails, where we pumped water from their well to wash the dishes. The water was then heated on the stove, where we washed everything in a porcelain basin and rinsed with the scalding water. The two youngest girls dried the dishes and put them away. It was a nightly custom that took about two hours.

I was surprised to learn that the Amish have no electricity. It grew dark after dinner where we retreated to a living room furnished with one faded sofa, five wood chairs, and two tables. A kerosene lantern provided the only light in the room. The smaller children played on the floor with handmade toys, while Mr. Yoder read from a small prayer book and Mrs. Yoder cut out fabric to make work shirts for her sons.

I was beginning to feel left out, when Elizabeth and the other two girls led me upstairs to the bedroom where I was to sleep for the next two months. I hoped the bed would be soft and comfy, like the one I had at home. I was surprised to see one double bed, with a patchwork quilt that was to hold all four of us!

We washed up in a pitcher and basin that was on a small wash stand. I then asked about the bathroom. The girls began to laugh, holding their hands over their mouths to conceal their glee.

We all proceeded to march down the steps and out of the back door from the kitchen to a tall wooden building that was called an outhouse, about fifty feet away on a worn path. A small, crescent moon was carved out of the top of the building. A full moon provided all the light we needed to efficiently do our business.

I peeked in the door and saw a long seat with a hole in the middle. Flies were buzzing about and a bad smell came from the inside. With a bit of prodding from my new friends, I carefully lifted my nightgown and sat down on this unfamiliar toilet. I wiped with the papers in a woven basket that sat next to me. I knew this practice was going to take some getting used to!

Headed back to bed, we all curled up together after we knelt and said our prayers. Since praying wasn't totally unfamiliar to me, I prayed for my mother to get well and for my father not to be sad and lonely.

It was a warm evening, with a breeze coming in from an open window. The cicadas were chirping and the frogs were croaking, in near perfect time. I couldn't remember hearing all those sounds back at home.

Since I was the newcomer, I was expected to sleep on the outside. I fell out of bed twice on the first night. I decided, after giving it much thought, that if I were to sleep at all, I had to sleep at the foot of the bed. With thirty little toes poking me through the night, I eventually fell asleep.

Morning came early in the Amish household. After a breakfast of hot oatmeal, cold milk, and fresh berries, Elizabeth and I were told that we were to gather eggs. It was a short walk from the house to the long, wooden henhouse. It sounded simple enough, but what I didn't know was that the mother hens would be sitting on their eggs in individual cubby holes, where they would peck at my hands as I reached under them to get the precious eggs. After my second attempt at getting an egg from one angry mother, I told Elizabeth I was afraid and my hand was bleeding. She smiled, took my hand and showed me how it was done. Show no fear, she would say. Let them know you're in charge; be firm and grab the egg! Surprisingly, her plan worked and I became quite good at it. Putting all the eggs into metal pails, we would trudge back to the house and deliver them to Mrs. Yoder. She never smiled when we finished a task, but I could always hear her quietly humming as we left the kitchen.

Since this was my first day at the farm, I was left to explore before lunch. There was a large, red barn with two stalls for the work horses, two outbuildings holding grain and corn, and the henhouse. I rounded the corner after exploring the barn, when I surprised a fat potbelly pig. He squealed and began chasing me, as I ran to the front porch. Mr. Yoder was coming in for lunch, when he saw me and scooped me up in his arms, a look of amusement on his face. One of the dogs came up to us, wagging his tail. Mr. Yoder put me down and patted him. I stood in the yard next to the dog, as he sniffed me and wandered off, finding me of little interest.

The summer wore on. My father faithfully came to visit every weekend, while all of us would sit on the front porch, drinking Mrs. Yoder's fresh lemonade. He assured me my mother was getting stronger every day and that made me happy.

Elizabeth and I had become good friends, and I considered her my big sister, since I was an only child. She was my special friend. All the other children were fun to be with, but it was like the kids in school. Only Elizabeth tried to make me happy. But she began to change toward the end of my stay, acting irritable and hard to talk to. She assured me it wasn't me, but I saw signs that she was having problems with her parents, and she would leave the house for long periods of time.

Finally, one night when the younger children were sleeping, she confided in me that she had met a boy-- not an Amish boy-- and that she loved him and they were planning to run off together. I wanted her to promise to come and visit me after they got married, but she said she couldn't. Because she was Amish, she could never come back. It was hard for me to understand that I would never see her again. I begged her not to go; that it was foolish to leave a family that loved her. I was glad it was dark, because I whispered that I loved her too. She listened to me and seemed content for a while. I thought things were actually back to normal in the Yoder household, but I was horribly wrong.

One late August night, when it was so hot I had trouble sleeping, I felt Elizabeth quietly slip out of bed, get dressed and leave the bedroom. I wondered why she was dressing, simply to go to the outhouse. Frightened, I went to the window, where I saw a young boy waiting for her. The moon provided all the light I needed. They kissed, took each other by the hand and quickly headed for the woods. I watched them as long as I could, before the trees swallowed them up and they were gone.

———

Colleen Grimes writes children's books and historical mysteries, as well as human interest short stories. She lives on a small horse farm in western Loudoun County Virginia with her husband, Mark. She has two grown children.

THE FIRST COVEN

P. M. Pevato

In a small cabin nestled in a forest high above a tiny mountain village, lived a woodcutter with his cherished wife and three lovely daughters. Even though the parents loved their daughters with all their hearts, the father longed for a son.

When the mother found she was expecting her fourth child, she was delighted, but suffered greatly the entire duration of her pregnancy. Sadly, when the mother delivered a healthy baby boy, she died in childbirth before hearing the wee newborn's cry. Their father wept for three months straight, unable to accept that his beloved wife was gone, leaving him alone to raise three young girls and an infant son. Soon, it was apparent that the girls were far too young to deal with the needs of a newborn, although the oldest daughter, Aradia, was mature for her twelve years. So the grieving man took his infant son to a village many miles away to be raised by his sister and her husband. When the father returned, he was even more despondent than before. Even though it was a sunny spring day, his sorrow cast a gloom like midwinter in the tiny cabin. Aradia realized that her father was still taking their shared tragedy very hard.

"Father," she said. "I know that you are heartbroken over the loss of your beloved wife, our cherished mother. And your only son is not here for you to see grow up in to a young man. Is there anything I can do to make your pain go away?"

"My dear eldest daughter," the father replied. "I only know of one thing that would make my days bright again. You cannot give me what I need. In fact, no one can ... I would wish my loving, beautiful wife could rise from the dead, and grow old with me. But alas, that is not possible, dear child."

Every morning, Aradia's father rose from his bed and sat at the roughly hewn table in the tiny kitchen. His breakfast of porridge, bread, and tea was set before him, but he barely ate. Unable to watch her heartbroken father continue this pattern day after day, Aradia became determined to find a way that would bring her mother back to life and grant her father's wish. Aradia was both clever and industrious. After her father left to gather wood and deliver it to the villagers far below their alpine cabin, Aradia went about her chores contemplating her project. How could she find a special recipe to bring her dearly departed mother back from the grave? Her mother had always found herbs and flowers in the forest that she used to cure all their ailments, and women from the village often came to seek her advice about a sick child or family member. Aradia was convinced that if she could find the right combination, she too could cure health problems—and what was death but the biggest health problem of all?

After telling her sisters that she had to gather herbs by the light of the full moon, Aradia set out into the forest. She was searching for herbs and wildflowers that might be combined to make a potion for her mother, whose freshly dug grave was in the family's graveyard behind the cabin.

"Dear child," said an old woman Aradia encountered on the forest trail. "You must try these magic herbs I have collected for you, in order to prepare your potion, for I know what you are planning."

"Thank you, Old Woman. Where are you from?"

But the old woman disappeared.

Aradia continued walking along the forest trail, humming a happy tune, until a large nine-tailed fox blocked her path. Aradia tried to scream, but the fox raised his paw in front of his gleaming teeth, as if to shush Aradia. "Silence, dear child, do not be afraid," the fox said. "I have collected magic wildflowers for you, for I know what you are planning, and you will need these plants."

"Thank you, Fox, I shall never forget your kindness. Where do you live?"

But the fox disappeared.

Once again, Aradia continued her journey upon the path, holding the herbs and wildflowers in one hand, and a lantern with a candle that illuminated the dark path. Suddenly, a raven swept down upon the path, digging its large claws into the pine needle strewn trail, and dropping a coal-like rock it held in its long beak.

The raven perched so as to be haloed by splintering rays of light from the Moon. "Dear child, you must use this magic rock in your potion. For I know what you are planning."

"Thank you, Raven, but how did you know?" But, just like the old woman and fox, the raven disappeared without saying another word.

A little later, the path led Aradia to a dilapidated hut with a crooked roof and an open door hanging by a single hinge.

"Hello? Anyone home?" When there was no reply, she took the already lit lantern from its hook beside the door and walked inside. There she found a huge black cauldron hanging above a freshly laid fire. She felt that someone had prepared the cauldron just for her.

Aradia sensed she must be on the right path.

***

For three nights, Aradia tiptoed out of her tiny bedroom in the cabin's cold attic she shared with her sisters, and returned to the hut with its cauldron. She spent many hours brewing her elixir by combining the magic herbs, wildflowers, and rock from the old woman, fox and raven. Then Aradia tested her potion on tree saplings and wildflower seedlings surrounding the tiny hut, pouring the elixir on the earth around the tiny plants. The very next day, to her great surprise, Aradia was met with a wall of soaring trees and blooming flowers around the hut, where she had tested her elixir. She was hopeful, but cautious. She knew many plants grew quickly and withered just as quickly. Aradia watched and waited. The weather soon turned cold in their high mountain forest, and fall announced the impending arrival of winter – yet the trees around the old hut remained green and defied the cold. The trees' ability to resist the little death of autumn convinced Aradia the elixir was ready.

The next time Aradia decided to venture from her tiny bedroom in the cabin's cold attic was All Hallows' Eve. She hurried to the hut with its cauldron, only to discover that her potion was gone. The cauldron was quite empty.

Aradia cradled her head in her palms and wept uncontrollably.

Only a folded note remained at the bottom of the dry cauldron. Aradia snatched it with one trembling hand.

Dear Aradia,

I apologize for my theft of your elixir. I have been watching you collecting and brewing ingredients. I even restocked your firewood for you, in case you had not noticed. To my delight, the young trees and infant flowers grew exponentially and blossomed overnight, and I knew that you had created the magical elixir. I congratulate you.

When I gave you the herbs of life and sent the fox and raven to you, I knew you had will and determination. I gambled my last remaining plants on the hope that you also had the unselfish purity of heart needed to combine them into the life giving elixir. I have no choice. I am very old and only the elixir can save me. Besides, the ingredi-

*ents were mine in the first place, and there was only
enough elixir for one.*

*Believe me, your mother will be better off in her grave
than living here on earth, for remember that life on earth is
fleeting, and death everlasting.*

Panic-stricken, Aradia ran out into the moonlight
night.

"Mother," she cried with her eyes raised to the
starry sky. "I have failed you on this night. The
potion that would have revived you is gone. For as
long as I shall live, I promise you, dear Mother, that I
will seek the magical ingredients and begin anew."

In her agitation, Aradia picked up a stick and
drew a series of lines, shapes and circles in the bare
earth before the door. These lines formed a strangely
symmetrical pattern over which the silvery light of
the moon shone. The pattern formed a star with five
points. Staring at the symbol she had inadvertently
created, she decided that the five points represented
the living members of her family, her father and his
four children.

Then Aradia drew another symbol in the middle
of the star, in the shape of a torn heart. "And this is
the heart of my beloved Father, broken irrevocably."

Finally, when Aradia drew a circle around the
symbol, she inhaled before describing aloud its
significance. "And this is the moon that shall
strengthen me when I am weak and need guidance."

Aradia searched in vain for herbs like those the
old woman had given her. When she felt her sisters

were old enough to know of her quest, she told them the story.

The youngest sister had an idea. "The old woman said there were no more plants, so we need to try something else. Mother left us her silver necklace with the gemstone the color of a ruby, set in the crescent moon. According to Father, our Mother polished this precious gemstone every night after she tucked us into our beds. Therefore, she may have left part of herself in the heart of this gem with her loving touch. Why not fill the cauldron with spring water from the twin falls behind our home, add the bloodstone to the cauldron, and see what happens?"

Aradia agreed unenthusiastically, but anything was worth a try. Later that same night, the three sisters left their cabin, leaving their father in a deep slumber.

Quickly, the sisters emptied jugs of spring water and waited until the fire roared and water bubbled. Then, Aradia carefully removed the stone from its setting, and tossed it gently into the cauldron. The bloodstone immediately shot bolts of fire, red and orange and yellow, out of the cauldron and turned the water crimson. As the potion boiled, the bloodstone rose out of the cauldron and hung suspended in the air above the cauldron. Aradia reached out and wrapped her fingers around the strange stone. The three sisters waited until sunrise, returning home before their father rose for work, carrying several jugs filled with the elixir, not taking any chances on its being stolen this time.

"How do we test this elixir?" the youngest sister inquired.

"There is only one way," Aradia declared. "We must all drink this potion together. As one. That is how Mother would have wished us to live ... or die."

Under the peaked roof of their cramped attic bedroom, the three sisters sat on the edge of their cots with small glasses in their hands. Aradia filled three glasses with the bloodstone potion. On Aradia's orders, they drank the potion together. And then settled down to wait.

Nothing happened immediately, but slowly so much changed. Aradia heard strange voices in her head, which seemed to be the unspoken thoughts of those around her. The middle sister discovered she could move logs and start fires with her mind. The youngest sister saw visions of faraway lands, though she rarely ventured out, and of faces she did not recognize. None of the sisters ever became ill, and if they had a cut or bruise, all healed quickly.

After a few weeks, they decided there was nothing to lose by trying the elixir on their dear mother. After all, she could only die once, right?

So one November evening, when the wind howled through the tall, sinewy trees and the moon cast burgundy shadows on the snow covered ground, the sisters set out for the tiny graveyard behind their cabin, where many generations of their ancestors were buried. Aradia held a lantern while her sisters surrounded the grave, and began to dig.

Suddenly, a well-known voice cried out. The startled girls dropped their shovels.

"What are you doing here so late at night?" It was their father, clearly not safely asleep as they had thought.

"Father, do not be afraid. For we have created a potion that will bring your beloved wife back to life. And you will smile once again, and be happy."

"No!" cried their father, throwing himself on his wife's exposed coffin. "You must not interfere with Death. Death will not be cheated. He will come for you instead, heed my warning."

"Nonsense," Aradia shook her head in disagreement. "I have already created a potion that overnight grows tiny saplings into majestic trees and mere seedlings into beautiful blooms. Except ..." her voice trailed off.

"Except what, my daughter? What else? Pray tell."

"Except my potion was stolen, and all the surrounding herbs and flowers I needed disappeared"

"So you are aware that there is a price to pay for interfering with Life and Death?"

"We have already paid a high price for Mother's death. She left us her rare bloodstone, as a piece of herself, of her heart, and she would be glad we have put the bloodstone to use," replied Aradia.

"Foolish girl, that bloodstone would give you financial security, not eternal life!" cried her father. "When I am gone, if you should not be secure in marriage, then you will have at least one valuable item to exchange for food and shelter."

"We have not harmed the stone," said Aradia, holding up her mother's precious gem that glistened in the moonlight, as dark as dried blood. "Nor will my sisters ever want for food or shelter, Father, this I pledge to you."

"And how will you put clothes on your back or a roof over your heads or food in your belly? You must either marry and be provided for, or go to work yourself. And you know there is no work for young uneducated women in the village below. I am a poor man, Aradia, unable to send you to school. I know I have not done all I can for you, but I have done my best. And I failed you because look what you have done, what you have become ..." he wept, shrugging his shoulders and holding his head in his hands.

"Father," Aradia said, placing her arm around his stooped shoulders. "How can you feel you are a failure? Your three daughters have learned many skills and crafts. We are talented, creative, and fiercely independent. We do not need to rely upon a man to provide us with food or shelter, when you are gone. Unless ..."

"Unless what, dear Daughter?"

"Unless you wish to drink a little potion and permit us to sprinkle some on Mother's decayed body — the decay that was once living flesh and bone?"

"Never! No! I beg you! Leave her rest in peace."

"But Father, after Mother's death, I asked what was there I could do to make your pain go away. And you said it was something I could not give you

... Mother rising from the dead, to grow old with you. However you underestimated me."

"What have you become, Aradia? My oldest, my first daughter, the image of my beautiful deceased wife?"

"I have not changed, Father. I am Aradia, your ever-loving devoted daughter."

"You have changed, Aradia, and you must leave my home at once. And I will cover Mother's coffin, where I too shall be buried one day. For I would rather join my wife in the afterlife now than anger the Spirits, Aradia. If you cross the Spirits, you will one day suffer," he warned.

"I am sorry you feel this way, Father, I only wanted ... wanted—"

"Yes, my dear Aradia, I understand. You wished Mother had never left. You must all promise never to disturb Mother's coffin again. Live a good life, and the Spirits will forgive you for what you have already done."

"I promise, Father. I am truly sorry. I thought you would be happy to be granted your only wish. But I was wrong. Goodbye, Father. I hope we shall be together one day."

Aradia snapped her fingers. In a cloud of gray smoke and flames the color of the setting sun, her father was blinded momentarily and shielded his face with his arms. When he opened his eyes, his girls were gone, just as the old woman and fox and raven had disappeared on the trail to the tiny hut. Gone,

205

too, were the bloodstone and the remaining elixir of life.

Very soon, the grieving woodcutter passed away and was buried next to his beloved wife. The three sisters returned shortly after his death. The villagers were too frightened to question their strange reappearance. The three sisters became known as the Coven.

The sisters developed their witchcraft over the centuries, traveling near and far and using their powers to help others. In respect for their father, they never attempted to bring back the dead. It is said that deep in the cold forest the Coven still returns to the small cabin, producing their elixir for new covens across the world. Where one finds bloodstone, one finds witches and the spirits that gave them their magic.

———

A flâneur *at heart, P. M. Pevato constantly seeks new experiences whilst strolling down the boulevards of life. Along this journey, the author earned degrees from Dalhousie Law School and the London School of Economics. For more, visit:* http://www.pmpevato.com *and her tumblr page* http://www.pmpevato.tumblr.com .

THE BIG SHORT

Jane Roop

Rich and arrogant, full of himself, Jasmine Oliver decided after reading the CEO's Letter to Stockholders. She needed to study the rest of the report if she was going to grill him the next morning but panting, moaning sounds of pleasure coming from the room next door made it hard to concentrate.

At seventy-five Jasmine still enjoyed the sight of tanned male shoulders and the exotic smell of male sweat. She closed her eyes and let her imagination roam over the joyful past. Her last husband, Bernie, had been so jolly and admiring. "Not much gets by you my love," he'd say with an appreciative gleam in his eye.

A sudden scream of pleasure or pain, she couldn't tell which, ended her stroll down memory lane. A signal it was time for her to either get back to LifeStream's annual report or wander down to the bar for a nightcap.

A nightcap seemed preferable. She grabbed her cell and room key. A thud, reminiscent of last summer's roofing project – a bundle of shingles tossed from the conveyer belt onto the roof – made her hesitate. The thin walls didn't provide much privacy.

When she heard the TV come on, she stepped in the hallway.

At that very moment, a stocky man of medium height in jeans and tan polo emerged from the room next to her. She noted the sockless feet tucked in brown tasseled loafers. She followed him to the bank of elevators.

Silver reflective sun glasses and a baseball cap pulled low covered most of his face, but nothing hid the missing joint of his right index finger as he tapped the ground floor button.

Interesting, she thought. Perhaps he was a logger or longshoreman. He had the burly, confident aura of someone at ease with physical extremes. Since he seemed totally unaware of her, she secretly angled the cell phone at her side and snapped a photo of his hand.

At the bottom, the man swerved left, and exited through the revolving doors.

She turned toward the bar and the soporific delights of bourbon on ice.

The TV in the next room played all night but was low enough she slept well. By 9 AM she was dressed, finished with prowling through LifeStream's audited financial statements and felt ready with hard-hitting questions. At the rate the company was losing money, its stock price would soon fall. Half of her inheritance from Bernie would be wiped out and the ample income from its dividends gone.

Downstairs in the foyer outside the Garden Ballroom, she first chatted with other stockholders, then helped herself to the lavish continental breakfast provided by LifeStream. She was mildly displeased at the excess expense, especially the flutes of champagne. What was wrong with a good glazed doughnut and coffee?

There was a sudden silence in the hallway.

A policeman and two ETs pulling a collapsible gurney caravanned to the elevators.

"What's going on?" she asked a stout woman next to her.

The woman shrugged, clearly more interested in her plate piled high with smoked salmon and cream cheese.

"I heard they found a woman, roughed up, drugged on the fourth floor, room 422, I think," said a tall, bald man on Jasmine's right. His plate, she noted with approval, was modestly full with fruit and a bagel.

"But that's right next door to me," she said.

"They'll be wanting to talk to you for sure," the man said.

Jasmine finished eating and found a seat near the front of the auditorium. The presentation began at nine, followed by a question and answer period. Being well prepared, she took her turn eagerly.

The CEO stood when the mike was shuffled down the line to him. He cleared his throat and took a sip of water. His oily, demeaning smile made her angry.

"As you know many of the strategies used by companies to hedge risk are highly complex, hard for anyone to comprehend," he started, "and best left to our capable investment advisors."

She might have missed the deformed index finger as he lifted his glass except for the TV monitors on either side of the auditorium.

"Hogwash," she snapped. "On pg. 30, footnote C, the company lost 25 million dollars. Please explain."

His answer was delayed by the noisy entrance of the hotel manager who scuttled down the aisle, up the stairs onto the stage, and whispered to the CEO.

"Unfortunately," the CEO said, "there's a problem in the hotel and the police are requesting our assistance. Would anyone staying on the fourth floor please meet in the Pine Room next door."

Jasmine walked to the edge of the stage and waved the CEO over.

"That includes you," she said.

"I'm not staying at this hotel." One nostril jacked up in disdain. "Don't mess with me granny," he hissed through clenched teeth. "You're an old bitch. Go home to your cats."

"You have no idea what an old bitch I am." She brought her cell phone up to eye level and tapped the picture on the screen. "Anybody you might know?"

A sharp intake of breath betrayed him.

"You should resign, today. Spend more time with your wife," she said, pivoted and left the room.

On her way to the Pine Room she called her broker.

"Jean I want to short 5000 shares of LifeStream."

"Mrs. Oliver that's a big, risky bet the stock is going down and street talk is it's going to report good earnings."

"I feel confident the price is going down."

"What are you doing?" Jean's voice took on a note of desperation.

"Squeezing lemons, dear, to make lemonade."

———

Jane Roop is a retired securities broker living in Kennewick, Washington, at the confluence of the Columbia, Snake and Yakima rivers.

THE INDIAN CURE

Sakeena Edoo

Even God had abandoned him!

Mohan sat holding the bottle he had just purchased. His last debt. This was his ultimate humiliation. He sat and contemplated his life, and what had brought him to this point. He had started adult life with such optimism and happiness. Yet now look at him. He could hear rustling some distance away and saw his five-year-old son coming towards him, bringing his lunch. He quickly wiped away the tears and hid the bottle behind his back.

"Papa, Papa," the child shouted, running towards him, with arms open wide, precariously balancing the tiffin box.

Mohan prayed he wouldn't drop it since he knew that it was the last handful of precious rice.

He embraced his son as tightly as he could, without knocking the wind out of him. He knew it would be the last time he would hold him. He gazed intently at the young, handsome, innocent face but he avoided looking into his son's eyes. He fought the tears that were threatening again. He stroked the child's head and hoped that this one action would convey the whole spectrum of fatherly love. His heart was breaking.

They sat side by side. He planned to feed the child as much as he could. Mohan had no use for food any more. He had no use for anything any more.

His culture, his upbringing, and even his whole psyche had stressed the importance of providing for his family. But here he was, unable to deliver on what was a man's ultimate role in life. What had gone wrong? Had he missed a glaringly obvious point somewhere? His head throbbed with all the unanswered questions. Never mind. It wouldn't matter soon.

He fed his son most of the food, while intermittently putting a few grains into his mouth so that the child wouldn't suspect. After which, they both settled into quiet reflection. He was grateful that his son had stopped chattering. Maybe he had sensed something different about his father that day. Maybe it was just the soaring, unforgiving heat that made him rest his head on his father's lap. They both contemplated the barren, three and a half acres of land, which stretched as far as the eye could see, that had once been Mohan's sufficient kingdom.

He reminisced about a time, which seemed a lifetime ago, when he sat like this with his own father.

"Mohan, all this will one day become yours. In India, when you own land you are a king. If you look after the land well, it will always look after you," his father had said.

All that changed, of course. Two weeks before his eleventh birthday his father died of tuberculosis, something that had plagued him since childhood. He and his mother farmed the land as best as they could. Until she had an accident and fractured her spine. He was nineteen years old. A few months after the accident his mother addressed the issue of marriage. In fact, she didn't address it, she laboured the point. He agreed that she would look for a girl for him to marry. He didn't have the heart to argue with her. A few weeks later, his bride had been found.

Her name was Abha, meaning lustrous beauty. She was everything, and more that her name promised. He had never seen anybody so beautiful.

Within two weeks of her family accepting his proposal, they were married. She came from an extremely poor family. So poor, that they waived the normal dowry requirements, in order for the wedding to take place. He was so excited. He was so happy. He was the luckiest man alive.

Sadly, his mother died four days after the wedding. He knew she had held on with every fibre of her being just to see him get married. He genuinely mourned the loss of his mother, while on the other hand feeling exuberantly happy about his wife. He was racked by guilt, he shouldn't feel this way. Yet when he glanced at Abha he couldn't help but be happy.

The timely monsoon that year ensured that his cotton crop was thriving, with no sign of the dreaded boll-worm, that could decimate a farmers' crop

214

almost overnight. The crop would be ready in a week's time and he would treat his beautiful wife with a new sari. Life was wonderful.

Mohan just got happier and happier. A year later his son was born. He held his newborn baby in his arms, brimming with parental love and pride. His life was just getting better and better. The crops were doing well, he and his wife got on extremely well, and now they had this bundle of joy to add to their family.

Their happiness lasted only two years.

Shortly after his son turned two, the dreaded boll-worm found its way into his cotton field. Overnight he lost the whole crop. Initially he tried to keep it from Abha, but she almost knew what had happened before he had told her. She was very calm and reassuring, insisting that something would happen to rescue them from their plight. He failed to be lifted by her outward confidence. He was also disturbed by a change he saw in his beautiful wife, she seemed distant and for some reason she couldn't meet his eyes. Maybe it was just his imagination. Maybe it wasn't. There was something very different about her from that day on.

They had a little money put aside, but their savings wouldn't last long. That night, his neighbour came to see him and told him about the new boll-worm resistant genetically modified cotton seed. A resistant seed sounded like a dream come true. At that point in time, the boll-worm was his biggest enemy.

The seed rep was going to be in the next village the following week. Mohan counted out his life savings and realised that he didn't have enough to buy the seeds with which to plant three and a half acres of land. That night he approached a money lender. The money lender refused, but said he would think about it some more and get back to him. Mohan was despondent. He didn't hear from the money-lender again.

The following week a neighbour came running.

"Mohan, Mohan, the seed reps are in the next village. Hurry, you might be able to catch them."

Mohan ran as quickly as his legs would carry him to the next village. He arrived puffing and gasping just in the nick of time. There sat the moneylender with the seed rep. It was the same moneylender that had refused to give him a loan previously. His heart dropped. Introductions were made, seeds discussed and loan agreed in the space of two minutes. The moneylender passed him a blank sheet of paper to sign. Apparently, the deal was done, and that was the contract!

"But it has nothing written on it," Mohan protested.

"Do you want the money or not? If you do, then sign, if not, go away and don't waste my time," the moneylender barked.

It took a further minute for the "contract" to be signed and the seeds, fertiliser and pesticide to be handed over. As Mohan left he looked back to see the moneylender rubbing his hands in glee, and the rep punching the air, while chanting "another one bites the dust."

This picture was chilling and disturbed him terribly. But he had no time to dwell on it. He had land to plant and a family to nurture.

***

In the ensuing three years, Mohan realised he had as good as sold his soul to the devil. All his hard work and toil just about put food on the table. The GM seed cycle had him trapped. He *had* to sell to the moneylender, and always at below the current quoted market price. On top of all this, Mohan paid five percent a month on the outstanding loan. He found it hard to comprehend how his fellow countryman could be complicit in destroying farmers, but this particular moneylender was fast becoming one of the richest men in the area. Not only from his innovative brand of usury, but the blank contract also enabled him to seize the land of anyone who defaulted on the payments.

Mohan was going over all this in his head, as he had done a thousand times before, when suddenly shouting jerked him out of his reverie.

"Uncle Mohan. Come quickly. Papa is ill," shouted a young boy, his neighbour's son. Mohan got up quickly, remembering to take the bottle that he'd hidden behind his back. He allowed his son to overtake him as they were coming up to a tree. He hid the bottle by the tree and continued running, praying that nobody would find the bottle.

They entered the neighbours' house, and Mohan could see that they were too late. His neighbour was wrapped in the chequered cloth that signified death, his wife kneeling beside him wailing.

"What's happened?" Mohan asked.

"He's killed himself." the neighbours wife replied.

"Why?"

"He couldn't get another loan to pay the four loans we've got. We are finished," she said, choking on her words.

Mohan helped the family prepare for the funeral. In the melee he had momentarily forgotten his son. He went to look for him and found him huddled in a corner by the chicken coop.

Hand in hand they walked home. Mohan hoped that his grip was giving his boy some comfort. He couldn't help reflect on an end to life that he had been planning for himself.

"Papa, Uncle Ji didn't love his family," said the boy.

"Why do you say that? Of course he loved his family."

"If he loved his family he would have never have killed himself. He has made his whole family unhappy, and he can never make up for it. You would never do something like that because you love us too much."

Those words were like a dagger being twisted in his heart. Maybe the child had a point. But how could a child understand or even comprehend what it felt like to have taken on three loans to buy seeds in one year. This year, waiting for a tardy monsoon, Mohan and the other farmers sowed their fields three times with the genetically modified seeds. Two batches of seeds went to waste because the monsoon was late. When the rains finally arrived, they came down so hard that they flooded his low-lying field and destroyed his third and final batch.

By the time he got home, Mohan was in an even greater state of turmoil than he had been that morning when he left. The decision was simple that morning, he was going to take a final debt of $9 to purchase a bottle of pesticide, he would drink that pesticide in the afternoon. Then it would all be over. The plan was simple. He hadn't banked on a conversation with a five year old to change his mind. Now his planned escape seemed selfish and short-sighted. What could he do? Sadly, love didn't put food on the table.

Mohan tossed and turned all night, having short fits of very disturbed sleep. He had thought he had found the perfect plan and only needed to execute it. Now he was back to square one. That morning he left as quietly as he could. He went and sat in his familiar place, surveying his land. He vaguely remembered a contorted dream about Gandhi that had taken place that night. What was it? Something about salt taxes? Yes. That was it.

Gandhi was one of India's most celebrated forefathers. He had taken on the might of British Rule and won. He had advocated and preached peace and non-violence in all of his campaigns. Mohan wasn't

219

sure he could advocate the same. Right now he wanted to go and murder the moneylenders and seed reps. But through his anger he saw that the solution might be to mobilise his fellow farmers in a coordinated protest.

He quickly ran and explained his plans to Abha. He was amazed that, though normally quiet and shy, she was enlivened by his idea. She offered to help him by going to talk to the villagers' wives. Between them, they decided to gather all the farmers together. After all, if Gandhi could do it why couldn't they? Historically, farmers had operated under the cooperative system, where they had looked out for each other and helped each other in times of need. The local silos had kept a percentage of grain for that exact purpose.

**

The following day the farmers gathered on his land. He started by quoting Gandhi.

"A small body of determined spirits fired by an unquenchable faith in their mission can alter the course of history," he said. "I have called you here today so that together we can farm our lands in the way we used to. India has been farming cotton for a lot longer than GM seed has been around. The bollworm has been around a lot longer than GM seed has. The monsoon has been around a lot longer than GM seed has. Yet never before have we been subjected to so much loss and deprivation. This is a new type of feudalism and it is happening because we are allowing it. Let us go back to the old cooperative system of farming. Will everybody who doesn't use GM seeds pledge to give a small proportion of his seeds to his neighbour? which will be returned at the next harvest. That way we can all boycott GM seeds in one go. If only a few of us do it, then they will bully us. If we all do it together, let's see what they can do."

Mohan was astounded and gratified by the response. They had agreed on a plan and they were all going to go back to traditional farming methods with traditional seeds. That one small action fired a backlash throughout India. Within weeks shock waves were felt around the world.

One Indian man's action took on the might of a large conglomerate that thought it was untouchable!

**

Three years previously ...

Jack's plans were working out to a T. He had been demoted to India because of a minor misdemeanour on his part in Washington. He hated the heat, he hated the dryness and dustiness and he hated the wetness of the monsoon season with a vengeance. In fact, he found very little to like in India. So he had decided he would break all sales records so that he could return to the States. This month he intended to earn the highest commissions globally, that the GM seed company had ever recorded!

He had been using his little blue box discretely and discriminately until the day he decided he wanted her. She was a shy little thing putting out the washing. When she saw him looking at her she half covered her face with the end of her sari and ran inside. She was beautiful. He had never seen such beauty on one woman before. Every feature of her face was sheer perfection. That coupled with her shyness and coyness made her irresistible. He had to have her. He watched her for a number of months and each time she saw him she ran inside. He had never waited for a woman so long. But this one was special.

That day he decided to hide behind a tree and wait for her. She had her back to him. He pounced from behind and put his arm around her waist. He nuzzled his face into her neck. She smelled divine. She wrestled out of his arms, turned and slapped him across his face and ran off. Wow! Jack hadn't expected that! He really thought she would just swoon into his arms.

The next day, he knew when her husband was out, he had watched for so long. He marched up to her house and calmly walked in, she was sweeping the kitchen. When she saw him, she straightened and got ready to run, but there was nowhere to go. He grabbed her arm and literally dragged her to his Jeep. There he opened the blue box and showed her the contents. She gasped!

Jack mimed his intent of spilling the box so that she would understand. Either he had her, or the whole box of boll-worms would be let loose on her husband's land. She understood. He dragged her back to the house.

She acquiesced.

What number was that then? One hundred and forty-nine. He needed one more to make one hundred and fifty sales this month. While driving away, he saw Mohan returning from his fields. He stopped by the field, took out his blue box and opened the lid. He watched as the boll-worms scurried around on the ground, with a satisfied smile on his face. This would be his ticket home!

———

Sakeena Edoo is a full time business owner. In her spare time, she is a freelance writer. She has written a number of children's books including books to help children deal with bullying. She is a single parent, with three children. Her entire career was in teaching or training.

GRANNY HITT

Lenora Rain-Lee Good

Granny, are you really taking the train to Chicago?"

"Yes, I am. I leave in four days."

"Why don't you fly?"

"I like train travel. Trains give one a chance to meet new people, and see the country. I have a roomette, so I can stretch out for naps and sleep in comfort."

"Well, I think I should come with you. You know, to help."

"Sally Anne, don't you *dare* turn into your mother! I may be 80 but I do not "dodder" nor do I need or want her help. When I do, I'll ask for it."

"But, Mother says—"

"I know perfectly well what your mother says. If she had her way, I'd be locked up in a nursing home, drugged until I die. If you're going to start behaving like your mother, I'll start treating you like I treat her."

***

Mary Anne, short, plump, rosy cheeks and sparkly blue eyes, looked exactly like everyone's concept of Mrs. Claus, complete with the square cut granny glasses. She had no problem finding her way onto the train. She also had no problem accepting the porter's help with her luggage. "After all," she told the porter, "age has its privileges." She slipped him a folded $10.00 bill as he left her room.

"Thank you, ma'am. You have a wonderful journey. Now, you be careful walking when the train is moving. Don't want to have to stop the train because you've fallen and hurt yourself."

"I'll be careful. Thank you."

"You can even have your meals delivered to your room so you don't have to leave at all. But, if you do leave, be sure to take your key. Have a very nice trip. And enjoy Chicago."

Mary Anne waited until the porter left and then began a leisurely tour of the car to see if anyone came aboard she might want to meet. She returned to her roomette before the train began to jerk out of the station.

"Good afternoon, Granny." The voice on her phone sounded like melted chocolate as he chuckled. "Are you in your roomette?"

"Indeed, I am. Thank you, it is very nice."

"Does it meet with your approval?"

"Oh my, yes. Very much. Thank you for arranging everything."

"Well, tell me, have you found Mr. Right, yet?"

"Yes, I believe I have. He's on the train, just a couple doors down from me."

"Good. Do you see any complications?"

"None at all."

"Wonderful. I'll call you when you're at the hotel."

What a strange way to make a living, thought Mary Anne. *But it pays well, for a minimum of work, and I do so love the fringe benefits.*

Mary Anne combed her silver hair, put it into a knot at the nape of her neck, refreshed her perfume, and made sure she had her room key before lurching to the door of her roomette. She headed down the hall toward the dining car. The train jerked and she crashed into the door of Roomette 12. Reflexively, as she fell onto the door, she grabbed the handle; it was not locked and she tumbled into the occupied room.

"Oh my! I'm so sorry. I lost my balance and when I grabbed, well, your door came open. Please, forgive me."

"It isn't everyday I have a good looking broad, I mean woman, literally fall at my feet." The man stood, and helped Mary Anne to her feet. "There. Are you all right? Do you want to sit for a bit?"

"Oh my, no, I'm fine, thank you. Just embarrassed. I'm on my way to the dining car, would you care to join me? The least I can do is buy you dinner and a drink, Mr...?"

"My name is Brent. Brent Jones. And yours?"

"Oh, I'm sorry, my name is Mary Anne. Mary Anne Hitt."

"Well, Mary Anne Hitt, I'd be delighted to accompany you to the dining car. Let me get my jacket and my inhaler...."

"You have asthma? I'm so sorry. I have perfume on. I hope it won't bother you?"

226

"No, not at all." Brent reached into his pocket and pulled out his inhaler. "It's just something I carry with me, in case." He smiled as he showed it to Mary Anne. "Canned air."

Once again, she marveled at how the Family always supplied her with the correct brand.

***

"Why, Mr. Jones, that was a delightful dinner; thank you for your company. I believe I'd like a brandy before turning in. Would you care to join me? Or will the smoke in the club car bother you?"

"I'm not fond of it, but if we sit away from it, well, I do have my canned air." He patted his pocket as he chuckled.

"Fine. I promise, I won't light up my cigar." Mary Anne smiled.

No one in the car was smoking, but the scent lingered from past patrons. Brent Jones used his inhaler. Mary ordered two brandies.

"Oh, my stars and garters! That was just what the Doctor ordered. I do believe I am ready to return to my roomette and sleep." Mary Anne stood. Brent stood, too.

"Yes, I think so. The brandy was delicious, and I thank you, ma'am. May I escort you back to your room?"

Brent saw Mary Anne safely to her room and did not notice when the train jerked and she bumped into him that she replaced his inhaler with the one she carried. Before Mary Anne closed the door he asked, "Would you care to join me for breakfast tomorrow?

About 9 a.m.? I enjoy your company."

"Oh, why, yes, I *would* enjoy that."

"I'll knock on your door at 9 a.m. sharp!"

Mary Anne put on her nightgown, slathered her hands with perfumed cream and put on her night gloves to hold the cream in, sprayed her hair with more perfume, put on her robe, then went to Brent's door and knocked.

"I'm so sorry to bother you, but do you have a 'Do Not Disturb' sign? Mine is missing, and I don't want the porter to knock on my door before I want to get up."

"No problem, Mary Anne. Here." Brent handed her his sign. She noticed he, too, was ready for bed. "Good night." He shut the door, wondering about little old ladies and why him?

"Good night, Mr. Jones. A very good night." She heard him wheeze, and imagined him using his inhaler. She returned to her room, placed the sign on her door, and went to bed with a good book.

No one knocked at her door at 9 o'clock. Mary Anne waited until 9:15. She stopped at Brent Jones's door, listened, heard nothing, knocked, waited, hung the sign on his door to return it, and went on to breakfast. She dined alone, as she knew she would.

She was in her hotel room when she turned on the TV and heard a man had been found on the train, dead, of an apparent asthma attack. The gentleman had at one time been connected to the Mob, testified against them and been in Witness Protection for several years.

228

Mary Anne smiled. The phone rang.

"Granny Hitt?" said the man with the deep chocolate voice. "Well done. A car will pick you up in two hours for your shopping trip. Enjoy. The driver will have your money."

***

"Honestly, Mother, I don't know why you took the train. They just aren't safe anymore."

"Sue Ellen, what are you talking about? Of course trains are safe. Why, I don't recall ever hearing of a train falling out of the sky killing all on board."

"Mother! For instance, that train you were on when you went to Chicago, well, someone *died* on that train. They think he might have been murdered."

"Really? I didn't see any police."

"Some old Mob guy in witness protection. They think he was killed."

"They *think* he was killed? Thinking doesn't make it so."

"Well, he was asthmatic, and his inhaler was defective. There was something wrong with it."

"That sounds to me like something from the manufacturer, not a murder. Honestly, Sue Ellen, you have a fit every time I take a trip. Speaking of which, I'm going to Europe in a few weeks. Live with it."

"Well, at least you won't take the train. You'll fly, like a normal person." Suspicion covered Sue Ellen's face. "Won't you?"

Mary Anne smirked, "Another cruise. On a ship. Then trains. On the ground." *I really shouldn't take such delight in baiting her, I know I shouldn't, but at my*

*age.... At her age.... At her age, I was a successful
contractor to the family business. Never once did I fail to
deliver despite a particularly maverick U.S. Marshal or
two making an occasional nuisance of themselves.
Especially that Tom character! Well at least that's what he
called himself on the cruise ship when he came
uncomfortably close to outing me.*

***

"Mother, don't you think it's time you started acting
your age? I mean, all this world travel and
gallivanting around by yourself. It's dangerous. What
if something should happen to you?"

"Sue Ellen, give it a rest."

Sue Ellen ignored her and continued on, "Besides,
it's costing a fortune. You're going to run out of
money, and —"

"Ah, that's the rub, isn't it? You're afraid I'll spend
all your inheritance, aren't you? Well, daughter mine,
I certainly intend to do my best at that." Mary Anne
laughed, which just upset her daughter even more.

"Now, tell me, how is Sally doing?"

"She's fine, Mother."

"How are her grades?"

"Four point oh. Why?"

"I'm thinking I may take her with me on my next
trip. If she doesn't have a passport, see that she gets
one, will you? That should make you feel better,
knowing she's with me, in case anything happens."

Sue Ellen sputtered. Try as hard as she might, she
could never fight her mother. It didn't matter how
much she tried to talk sense to her, Mary Anne did

whatever she wanted. And now she wanted to take Sally on one of her horrid trips. Not for the first time did she bewail the fact her family did not meet her expectations of normalcy. "It's Daddy's fault. He should never have taken you on so many trips."

Sally accompanied Mary Anne to Buenos Aires. They flew first class, spent a few days shopping, and then took a cruise to Antarctica. It wasn't until after the ship returned to Buenos Aires that it was discovered one of the passengers had not disembarked. A thorough search of the ship turned up nothing — no note, no nothing. Anti-depressants found in his stateroom led the authorities to believe he committed suicide by jumping overboard, though nothing showed up on any of the surveillance tapes. There was one place where the camera angles didn't overlap. He walked from one camera toward the next, never to be seen again. Sally and Mary Anne walked the same route, moments after he did, and told the authorities they saw nothing. "Oh my, how horrible. Was it quick, do you think? I mean, going into that frigid sea?"

The police felt great sympathy for this fragile old lady and her young granddaughter. What an awful thing to remember from an otherwise flawless adventure. "Yes, ma'am. We are confident it was quick. Thank you for your cooperation. Please enjoy your stay in Argentina and do not think again of this incident."

Sally began to accompany Mary Anne on her trips. The trips were planned so as to not interfere with

Sally's classes. Sally maintained her four point oh
and graduated with an MBA. She had a short vaca-
tion after graduation before going to work for a large,
family-owned business. When her grandmother
became ill and went into Hospice at Park West, Sally
spent most of her off duty time helping to care for
Mary Anne. Her bosses were very generous in
allowing her time off for that purpose. They understood the meaning of Family.

"Granny," Sally excitedly told Mary Anne, "you
have a visitor down at reception. He says he met you
on a cruise a long time ago — his name is Tom. Said
he was in hardware?"

"Yes, dear. Bring him in. My, a gentleman caller.
At my age." Mary Anne smiled.

"Why, hello there, Little Lady." Sally watched as
this strange man with the phony accent looked at her
granny and tried to hide the shock of seeing her so ill.
He hid it behind a huge bouquet of her granny's
favorite flowers, which he placed on the dresser so
she could see them. When he turned around, Sally
noticed his composure was in place.

"Oh my stars and garters! Why, hello, Tom. What
a nice surprise!" She turned to her granddaughter
and said, "Sally, why don't you go down and make
us each one of those frozen fruit drinks. I'd like
pineapple. Tom, what would you like?"

"Oh, Little Lady, I think I'm fine." Tom smiled a
rather sad smile.

"Why, I insist. She makes very good ones. Or,
would you prefer a chocolate shake? She makes great

shakes, too." Sally caught the quick smile he gave at the mention of a chocolate shake and quietly left them alone.

She returned with their drinks, handed Tom the chocolate shake and Mary Anne the pineapple smoothie. "Sally, why don't you go on and get your dinner. Tom will be here for a bit, and if I need anything, he can call a nurse. Go on, now. Scoot."

"Little Lady, I mean, Mary Anne, I haven't been all that truthful with you."

"Oh. Oh my, it couldn't be that phony John Wayne 'Little Lady' bit that wore thin the first time you used it, could it?" Mary Anne smiled. He looked every bit the professional cop, a far cry from the pathetic, bore of the cruise, but then he'd been undercover at the time.

Mary Anne sipped her frozen drink. Tom took a swallow of his chocolate shake and then quickly two more. "This is the best chocolate shake I've ever had. Did she make it, or is it a mix?"

"Oh, oh no, she makes them. I don't know what she puts in them, but they are good. I can't have the milk any more, but I do get so hungry for them. It's nice to watch you drinking, and enjoying, one." She smiled a genuine smile at Tom.

"Little Lady, I mean, Mary Anne, I'm a U.S. Marshal." He showed his badge and identification to Mary Anne. "We've been investigating you for a long time and when I found out you were here, in Hospice, I asked to come see you."

"A U.S. Marshal? Investigating me? Oh, my.

Whatever for? I don't understand." Mary Anne batted her blue eyes in feigned innocence.

"Mary Anne, you must know that wherever you travel, people die."

"Why, Tom, people die all the time. Just yesterday, Charlie in the room next to mine died. And last week, Agnes, across the hall died."

"That's not what I mean, and you know it."

"Why, I'm perplexed, Tom. I truly am."

"You're good, Mary Anne. One of the best operatives I've, shucks, *we've* ever encountered. You're dying. Why not give a dying declaration, now. Clear your conscience. Go to your Maker with a happy heart. We've noticed that all the men who have died, more or less in your company, were all in Witness Protection. Give us names, Mary Anne. It's time to put an end to it. Tell me, how do your bosses find them?"

"Goodness, Tom, you're better as a hardware salesman! I declare I haven't the foggiest notion what you're talking about."

"Mary Anne, we know you work for the Mob, or the Family, as you call it. Look, I checked your records and you've got days, at most a couple weeks. They can't get you now. Help us. I'm begging, Mary Anne. Help us. Give us names. Give us data we can use. It's time to end this. If you're worried about your family, we'll protect them."

"I'd be most happy to, if I knew what you wanted. But I just don't understand any of this conversation." Mary Anne began to cough. When she finished

234

coughing, she lay back on her pillow, visibly tired. "Thank you so much for coming. If you leave your card, I'll have Sally send you the recipe for the shake. Now, please, I need to rest." Mary Anne closed her eyes in sleep. Resigned and frustrated, Tom left the room. The sadness in his heart, however, was genuine. He rather liked the old gal.

"Sally, would you take those flowers down to reception?" Mary Anne pointed to the bouquet Tom brought. "I think I'm allergic to them."

"Yes, Granny."

Sally wore a big grin as she returned to the room. "I threw them in the dumpster. Good thing, too. There was a bug right in the middle of all those pretty flowers." Mary Anne smiled as Sally continued, "Oh, I think we might want to watch the news. It seems the gentleman who came to visit you earlier today was involved in a fatal accident as he turned left out of Park West. They think he had a heart attack while at the wheel and pulled out into oncoming traffic."

———

Lenora lives in the high desert of Washington State where she writes poems, novels, and radio plays. When not writing, she reads, quilts, makes jam, and takes road trips. Her novel, Madame Dorion: Her Journey to the Oregon Country, *is published by S & H Publishing. See* https://www.facebook.com/MadameDorion

RICKESTMORTAPHOBIA[10]

Krisi Keley

I can't say that I'm fond of sailboats. In fact, I suppose I must admit to having a pathological fear of them. I call it Rickestmortaphobia because, apparently, there is no specific designation for this particular fear. Aqua or hydrophobia is the fear of water, but my phobia is not so all-encompassing as that. I love baths, for instance, as I can never feel clean enough. That I can't is related to my Rickestmortaphobia; but I guess that you, my Irony-Deficient Therapist, won't find me making note of this any funnier than you find my fear of sailboats. Hence your advice that I write this supposedly therapeutic "purge." Obviously, you find your made-up words and concepts more acceptably witty than my own.

So here is the "purge," O Great Curer of Ailing Minds. I doubt seriously that it will keep me from running screaming from the room the next time one of my fellow sedated inmates draws a crude portrait. I mean, if something that resembles a brown half-moon knocked on its side, with a really tall version of the astronauts' "we were here" flag sticking up out of

[10] Originally appeared on http://www.cleverfiction.com as "The Purge", 2011.

it, is enough to set my teeth on edge, just how this foray into psychoanalytic creative writing will save me, I honestly can't imagine. But if you insist that it will work wonders with those who hold the key to my nuthouse cell door, then who am I to question your experience? So here is my experience, which I shall entitle: A Short History and Analysis of Rick-estmortaphobia.

A thousand years ago, to celebrate my twelfth birthday, my stepfather, Rick, announced to my mother and me that he was taking me sailing. "What a treat!" my ever-blind mother exclaimed with enthusiasm, while I begged her with my eyes that there was no birthday present I wanted less. But my mother had had this sight impairment for years and my silent pleading this day was no more effective than it had ever been. So off set Rick and I on our sailing adventure from the Jersey shore. My stepfather, apparently emboldened by my now more adult age, seemed to decide that the "love" he usually expressed for me in the privacy of my bedroom while my mother — hearing as well as sight-impaired — slept the sleep of the dead, could be shown in places more public. Was his not noticing the gutting knife kept on the sailboat for the lucky fishermen who reeled in a big one a boon or a curse for me? Well, that all depends on how one looks at things. Because when he tried to bestow his affection on me this time, he became the unlucky fish.

I can't say that it was unintentional, but then, it is hard to remember what I meant or did not mean to do. Years of his monstrous presence darkening my existence coalesced into one all-consuming terror in that instant, so I reacted without thinking at all. Or at least, it seemed so to me. Certain that no one would believe me or understand, I did mean to push his body overboard, although it is still hard to consider this premeditation. Remember that even my own mother had never believed me or understood. So was it really so strange that a twelve year old would be convinced that neither would the rest of the world? What I didn't foresee was that Rick, still clutching my blouse in his literal death grip, would pull me with him, tipping the boat and spilling us both into the water. But whether my Rickestmortaphobia really started that day — the day I was almost physically killed by my dead stepfather, similar to the way I'd been emotionally and spiritually murdered by the live one for years — is debatable. Instead, it might have begun with the nightmares that followed. Those which arrived every night after I was questioned by police and those which continued throughout the hearings held to decide what punishment might fit the crime of a minor who stabbed to death her "allegedly" molesting stepfather. Or maybe it was born of the nightmares that came after my mother testified against me, swearing her "beloved" and upstanding doctor husband would never do such a thing and that I'd always been a wild and incorrigible child.

In any case, O Healer, this is why I run screaming from even only pictures of sailboats, while water...

water, I love. The baths I take repeatedly to cleanse me of my stain—the ones Rick left on my body as well as the one I carry on my soul. And the rain that I sometimes dance in when allowed to have supervised outings... that is the proof of my shame and contrition, as much as it is the tears I dare to think God cries on me from Heaven, I pray with the forgiveness and compassion and understanding my mother and the court who exiled me to this "healing" facility did not show me. The reason sailboats will always be my fear, but water...that will always be my hope. And the real purge that this therapeutic reliving of my phobia's birth can never be.

Sincerely, your patient on her eighteenth birthday, Kate.

———

Krisi Keley, an author and artist, lives in Chester County, PA with her family and her dogs. The first two novels of her Friar Tobe Fairy Tale Files, Mareritt *and* Vingede *are published by S & H Publishing, Inc. Her other series,* On the Soul *can be found on Amazon as well.*

A LESSON IN LOSS

Caroline Doherty de Novoa

Miguel and his family have spent months at the
hospital. Well, at least to a five-year-old it feels
like months; maybe it is only a few weeks. When he
is tired he sleeps on the plastic chairs in the visitors'
room with a cushion brought from his grandmother's
sofa. The chairs are the same pale, lifeless green as
the doctors' uniforms.

His grandmother's two maids make huge vats of
food that they bring to the hospital to feed the family
who gather there each day. Even his uncles come
from their offices to eat with the rest of the family at
lunchtime. Assembled in the visitors' room, they look
like any typical Colombian family out for a picnic, his
uncles telling jokes and going back for seconds, the
teenage cousins fiddling with their gadgets and the
women gossiping. He notices other families staring at
them, but no one else in his family seems to notice or
care. The maids make everyone's favorite food:
hearty stews, beans, thick soups; all dishes typical of
Antioquia, the region where his grandmother grew
up. She oversaw the training of both of the maids to
make sure they knew the recipes of her mother and
her grandmother to the exact half teaspoonful measure of salt or spice. She never got around to teaching

these recipes to her only daughter, who now lies dying a few doors away.

The illness has transformed his mother. She has lost her thick dark hair and now wears colorful scarves to brighten up her appearance. Otherwise, with the exception of her emerald eyes, she is devoid of color. Her eyes are starting to fall deeper into her face, encircled with skin so dark it looks like charcoal next to her white cheeks. But otherwise her eyes do not change. They still shine out from within the black circles as beautiful as always. When he becomes frightened by all the physical changes, when he feels he does not recognize his mother in the woman lying pale and lost in the huge hospital bed, then he focuses on her eyes, and there she is again in front of him, the mother who reads him bedtime stories, the mother who took him to his first day at school and waved him off on his first weekend away with the boy scouts.

The cancer has robbed her of all physical strength. She used to be able to swing him high over her head. He loved soaring above her in a fit of giggles, so safe and free, but now she barely has the energy to lift a newspaper. His father turns the pages for her and folds them to make it easier for her to hold. She dispenses with each page quickly. She says she only has the energy to read the headlines and look at the photos. She does not have enough time left to bother with the detail. His father jokes that she only ever looked at the pictures, anyway. He loves the smile that his father's jokes bring to her face. It gives her energy from an unknown source, bringing back the color and the light, if only momentarily. He wishes he could have the same power to bring someone back to life with a simple joke.

Though one joke frightens him. He is playing in the corner of the room and his parents do not realize that he is listening.

"I'm afraid that I'll get eaten by worms. You know of all the crazy things, that's what gives me nightmares. I'm such a fool," his mother says.

"Well, don't worry about that," he hears his father say, "we'll just burn you instead. Problem solved." And there is that smile again. This time she even manages a spontaneous laugh and a playful slap for her husband—done before her body remembers that it does not have the energy for such mirth.

Miguel is confused. He doesn't understand why she is afraid of worms. The hospital is clean; there is no soil anywhere. He checks the potted plants, but they are plastic, held into their pots by foam. He follows his uncle outside when he goes to smoke a cigarette.

"You won't burn her, will you?" he asks. "You'll be careful with your lighter."

***

As his mother gets weaker, the family spends more and more time in prayer. His grandmother leads the rosary three times a day at six-hour intervals in the visitors' room. Miguel copies everyone else and lowers his head as his grandmother races through the first half of the prayer, not stopping for breath. Then he hums the second half with the crowd. He doesn't know the words, although he isn't sure if anyone knows the words or if they are all just humming along hoping not to get caught out. In the beginning, his father gets annoyed with all the praying and storms out.

"This is what they do at funerals. My wife is not dead. She is down the hall and can hear you."

His father's lack of faith is a constant source of conflict with his maternal grandmother, but eventually as the weeks pass, he starts to join them for prayers. The women on their knees, with straight backs and eyes out in front of them, look like they are conversing with God as equals, but his father looks like a beggar, crumpled and desperate, with no other option than to bow down and beseech the kindness of a greater power. He hopes his father can make a pact with God and they can keep his mother here on earth.

Playing quietly in the corner of his mother's room as she sleeps, eating and praying with the family in the visitors' room, telling jokes to the nurses, making friends with the other children that visit, all becomes routine, normal.

**

One day his aunt comes with his two cousins to pick him up after school. She hugs him tightly as she says hello. Her face looks different. Her eyes are heavier, swollen, she is not wearing any makeup. She tells him that they are not going to the hospital for lunch, that she is taking him and his cousins to the mall for

243

hamburgers and to play in the arcade. Miguel asks when he will see his mother.

"Later, darling, you will see mama later. She wants you to be out having some fun." But they don't go to the hospital that evening. Instead, his aunt takes him home with his cousins for a sleepover. She lets them stay up late watching videos and orders pizza for dinner. His uncle comes home very late, after Miguel and his cousins are in bed. The door is slightly open and he can see his aunt and uncle embrace, his aunt holding her husband close, rocking him back and forth.

Miguel is frightened and cannot sleep. He lies in bed focusing on the small slit of light coming in from the doorway. He doesn't understand why he hasn't seen his father and mother all day. His aunt and uncle seem so different, they are behaving so strangely. It is like all the adults are lost.

In the morning, his grandmother comes to the house. Seeing her immediately makes him feel more secure; she is always in control. She tells him that they are not going to the hospital, they are going to the funeral home. She explains that that is where they take people when they have died and asks if he understands what that means. He nods. He has seen people die on TV, they become still and their eyes close and people are sad. His grandmother explains that his mother's body is asleep at the funeral home but her spirit has gone to be with God. She explains that the spirit is the part that makes a person who they are, it is the part that loves, it is the part that speaks and laughs and creates and remembers. His aunt leaves the room in tears and his grandmother helps him to get dressed.

***

The funeral home is not a house. It is a big official-looking building with a steep marble staircase and shiny wooden doors. His uncle carries him up the steps, and on the second floor he takes him into a big, dimly lit room filled with fold-out chairs. People sit whispering in small groups. A ghostly murmur hovers in the air. In the corner of the room, hundreds of flowers are crowded together, like a secret garden hidden in the middle of this cold and polished building, their perfume overwhelming. In the middle of the flowers rests a long wooden box on two stands. He sees his father kneeling down next to the box like an abandoned child, scared and alone.

His grandmother nods for him to go to his father. Miguel walks over tentatively, terrified of what will happen next. His father reaches for him, clings to him with all his strength. Suddenly Miguel, too, is crying, uncontrollably.

The rest of the day is a blur. He doesn't understand the resignation of the adults. To him death is like the bogeyman; it sneaks in during the middle of the night and steals your spirit away from inside of you, squeezes it into an empty jam jar and leaves behind the empty body. He doesn't understand why his mother had waited at the hospital for death. He's angry that she didn't hide away somewhere safe.

The next day, hundreds of people gather in church to pray for his mother. But even the prayers of hundreds do not bring back her spirit, so they take the box that contains her body and bury it. He remembers at school they had planted a bulb in the ground, too, and a few months later it blossomed into a flower, so he believes that they are storing her body safe in the ground until they are able to recover her spirit from death. Then she will reappear like the flower, her frozen body warm again.

Only months later will he realize that death is a permanent separation, and he will mourn her again, crying in his grandmother's arms for hours.

***

On his fifteenth birthday, his grandmother presents Miguel with a letter. It is from his mother, written shortly before she died, a note really, scribbled in a lazy script inside a card with a picture of some red roses on the front: *"I've been going over and over in my head what I want to say to you in this letter. It is my only link to you in the future and I could write a novel if I had the time. But I know my time is nearly up, so what to tell you, son? What is important? Walk through life with your eyes open. Be conscious. Make your own decisions and believe in yourself. Live life passionately to the end.*

Death is just the moment when living stops. If you have lived, then Death can hold no fear for you. But some people stop living long before Death, some never even start. That is the real tragedy. I wish I could tell people how nice it is to die of cancer because I now see Death up ahead and I know that I am living. Cancer, with all its indignities, has shown me my beautiful life – which I will squeeze and hold onto until the end. Live your life like that, son. Every day look Death in the eye and rejoice in your glorious life."

———

Caroline Doherty de Novoa grew up in the Northern Irish countryside. Over the years, she has called Manchester, Madrid, Oxford and London home. She now lives in Bogotá, with her husband Juan. She is the author of "Dancing with Statues", a novel set in Northern Ireland and Colombia. See www.carolinedohertydenovoa.com.

DOESN'T MATTER[11]

Ian Lahey

Mind you, I'm not so worried that this might wipe out the whole universe. I *am* a bit bugged by the fact that it's us causing it. "

"Nonsense," Professor Whymward replied to his whining assistant, "and in any case, if it happens, it won't really matter will it? Nobody there to blame us." He flashed a comedian's grin.

Dipak Singh didn't seem to enjoy the humor. "It won't matter because matter won't exist, you will have been responsible. How can you live with such guilt?"

"I won't. Anyway it won't happen, my experiment is perfectly safe. Now help me with the plutonium case, it's the one with the handles on the sides."

Still muttering to himself, Dipak went to the far side of the lab, which was full of dusty equipment, vials, and a pyramidal pile of computers stacked chronologically like geological strata. The case was on the floor next to it. He grabbed the heavy box with the black and yellow markings and set it on the lab table while Whymward just barely made room for it by quickly removing his tablet and tossing it on the

---

[11] An earlier version of "Doesn't Matter" participated in a short story competition on http://www.mywriterscircle.com.

computer pile, where it landed neatly over the professor's previous favorite, a notebook pc.

"In any case matter doesn't really exist anyway," Whymward went on, apparently driven by the momentum of the argument, "that's precisely what I intend to prove. And I will prove it, to you and to the committee. What time is it?"

"Quarter to twelve."

"Excellent. We just have time to set it up before lunch, and then we'll be ready for them. Radiation suits."

"Yes." Arguing with the professor had never led to anything good, and a position as assistant these days was truly a blessing. As Dipak put the clumsy suit on, he thought of his wife and his seven children. Losing the job because of a disagreement was out of the question. Anyway, Professor Whymward knew best. After all, isn't that what a professor is, a blooming know-it-all?

A few minutes later they were leaving the lab. Whymward gave Dipak a congratulatory and painful slap on his back.

"We're gonna blow their minds, one way or another, eh old boy? Remember to lock up now, word has begun to go round the faculty and I want nobody meddling with our equipment." Then off he was, rushing towards his usual lunch ritual: sandwich, light salad and post-it notes.

Dipak Singh stood there with his head bowed and his hand on the half turned key.

The Committee for the Investigation of Scientific Claims had been selected, apparently, with the exclusive intent of annoying the professor. Most of them looked like they'd been dragged out of a retirement home just before their favorite TV shows.

Whymward's initial presentation had gone relatively well, for a full thirty-five seconds, up to when he declared his theory on matter.

"If matter doesn't really exist, fall through your chair!" one of the elderly members called out.

"I can't," Whymward replied, "the chair contains information that prevents me from doing it. You see, that's-"

"How can it contain something if there's no container?" another one interrupted.

"There's information on that too! Listen, all of our studies on matter regularly come up with nothing but information. You call them 'particles' and are puzzled by how they look like matter but never have any mass, and it's nowhere to be found, and you know it. Professor McMahon, you worked with the Large Hadron Collider until what, five years ago? Did you find anything?"

"No we didn't, but we will! We just need to look harder!" McMahon slammed his walking stick on the floor.

"No, you won't because there is no matter!" Whymward shot up from his chair and stood in front of the board. "It doesn't exist! It's just data, information, instructions! The source code of the universe!

And today I'll prove it!" By now the professor's face had gone from healthy pink to an ugly blotched red.

There was a moment of silence punctuated by the quiet rattle of pill bottles. Dipak sat in silence, hoping the course of events would now turn towards a less dangerous ending, perhaps a nice brawl.

"How are you going to do that?" The president of the committee finally asked.

"It's really very simple." Whymward returned to his seat, his complexion once more relaxed. "Well no, it's horribly complex in fact, but the idea behind it is simple: To prove all is made up of information, I'm going to change a very small bit of it. This will alter reality slightly but noticeably."

"Hah!" was all the President could say. The others now looked at the machinery in front of them with the same expression Dipak knew from his own mirror. They were thinking about the risks. But there was no turning back now.

"Without further ado, here we go, for the next minute I ask you to concentrate on your surroundings and your perception of them, it may be anything, from the sudden alteration of time to a missing button in your shirts. Dipak, if you will."

Hesitating, feeling the Committee's eyes on him, Dipak reached for the switch and activated the device. There was a loud hum, a pop and a soft 'parp' like a balloon deflating.

A minute passed. Slowly, like the tide rolling in, grins started appearing on the faces of the Committee.

"Still got ten fingers."

"Wristwatch still ticking."

"Wife's still texting nags."

Professor Whymward looked at the chuckling old men, then at the device and finally at Dipak, who stared back, blankly.

"Dipak..."

From the tone of voice alone the assistant knew it was all over for him. He tried to defend himself. "I -"

"Traitor! You sabotaged the machine! I wasn't going to destroy the universe!"

"I didn't -"

"Out! Get out!" the red splotches had returned. Dipak left the room, there was no way in the world he could have proven his innocence. As he was walking back home he thought about his wife, then about Ajit, Aseem, Kumar, Chanda, Yaya, Meera and Candace. His steps slowed down, he just couldn't face them without some internal support, so he deviated towards the nearest pub.

It was close to midnight when he stumbled out of the pub, half drunk. He was not surprised to see his wife waiting for him.

"Nisha, I'm sorry. I lost-"

"Shh! Look!" His wife pointed both at the large clock on the wall and the small digital one on the table.

Dipak looked. He stood in open-mouthed astonishment and counted all thirteen chimes as the hands clicked to the upright position.

———

252

Ian Lahey was born in Milan, Italy, to an American father and an Italian mother. He teaches English Literature and Aviation English in Udine and leads a quiet and ordinary life with his wife, his two children and his invisible cat, Laurelin. To learn more about Ian, visit his FB page: http://www.facebook.com/lovewritingstuff.

DID YOU ENJOY THE BOOK?

MAKE THE AUTHORS HAPPY

LEAVE A REVIEW!

S & H Publishing, Inc. is proud to publish this and other books by many of these very talented authors. Visit us at http://sandhpublishing.com

Made in the USA
Middletown, DE
26 November 2014